T0164818

Arsinoe of Ephesus

Lorraine Blundell

AuthorHouse™
1663 Liberty Drive
Bloomington, IN 47403
www.authorhouse.com
Phone: 1-800-839-8640

First published by AuthorHouse 05/25/2011

ISBN: 978-1-4567-7660-2 (sc)
ISBN: 978-1-4567-7661-9 (e)

Printed in the United States of America

This book is printed on acid-free paper.

Dedication

For my son Steve and my daughter Jenni without whose love, support and patience over many years, this novel would never have been written.

A special thank you to Jenni for being the most wonderful travelling companion anyone could wish to have.

Acknowledgements

Firstly to the lovely Lauren, thank you for your support and being so positive about my writing. Susan Shorter, thank you for an exquisite front cover illustration.

To Jenni, my thanks for all of the photos, maps and help with computer input.

To Tarek Mostafa, Egypt, what a wonderful tour of a country blessed with incredible sites without equal. Thank you, Tarek, especially for your guidance through the Temple of Isis at Philae! This is one of the rare places In the world, where I believe it is possible to experience the emotions expressed in the novel by the character of Cleopatra, during her visit there.

Finally, but not least, to Barcin Taran, my experienced and highly knowledgeable guide of the sites in Turkey. Thank you for Sardis and Hierapolis, but especially for the tour of Ephesus. You brought the everyday world of that ancient city to life, as well as locating Arsinoe's tomb for me. I have you to thank for igniting the spark of inspiration to write this novel.

Any errors or omissions are, of course, my own.

The Moving Finger writes; and, having writ,

Moves on: nor all thy Piety nor Wit

Shall lure it back to cancel half a line,

Nor all thy Tears wash out a Word of it

The Rubaiyat of Omar Khayyam

Quatrain 51

Ptolemy Dynasty Family Tree

The Claim to Egypt's Throne

'Ptolemy XII had six children... the last two each ruling briefly with Cleopatra VII. The identity of Cleopatra VII's mother is not certain.'

1.9. Strabo, '*Geography*.' 17.1.11

Strabo, (BC 63 – AD 24)

Greek Philosopher and Historian

Cleopatra VII's paternal grandfather was Ptolemy IX

The identity of her paternal grandmother and maternal grandparents are not clear

ANCIENT SITES

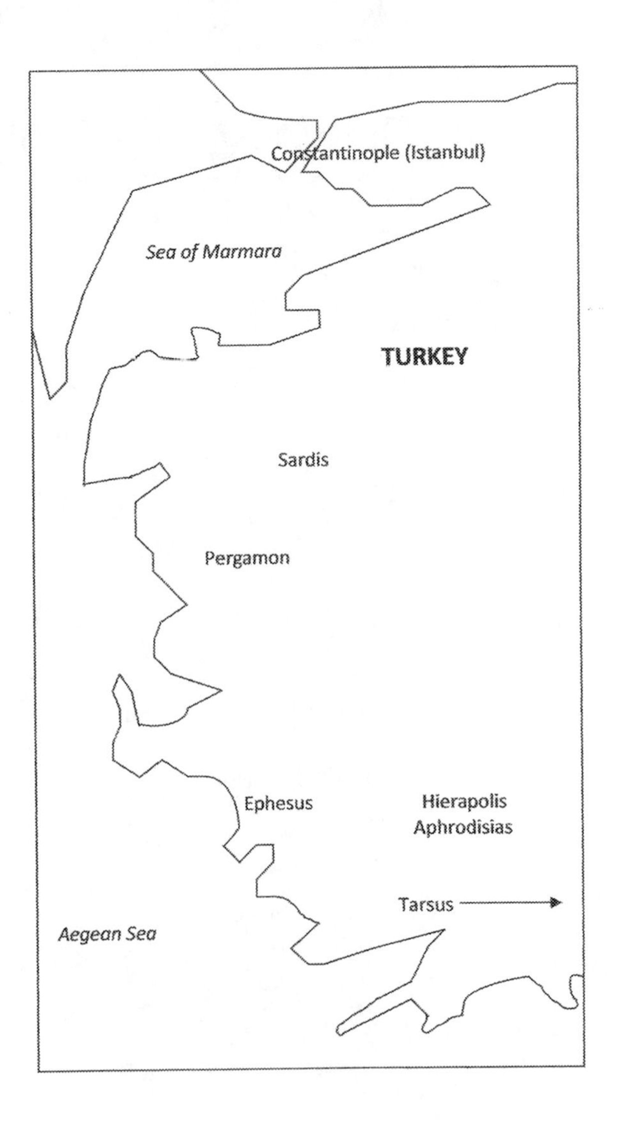

Ancient City of Ephesus

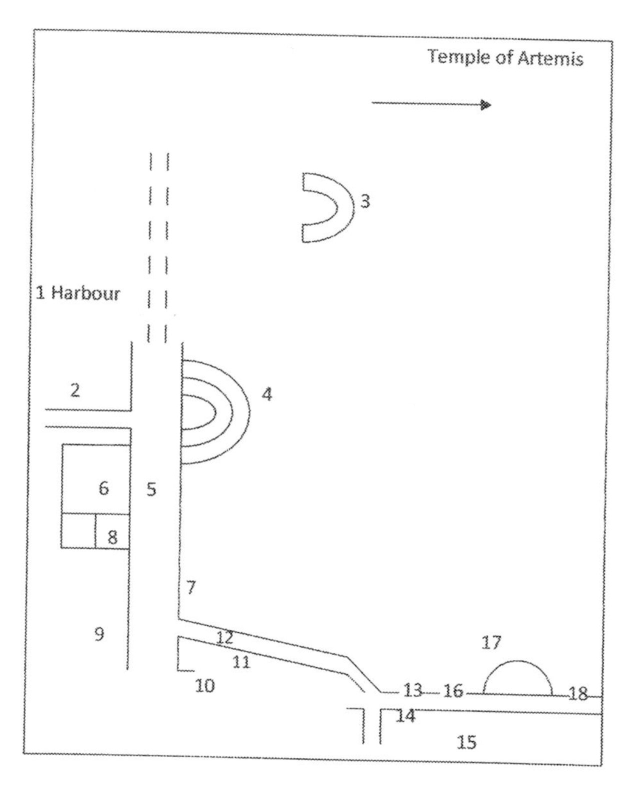

1. Harbour
2. Arcadian Street
3. Stadium (Hippodrome)
4. Theatre (Great)
5. Marble Street
6. Lower (commercial) Agora
7. Brothel
8. Gates of Mazeus and Mithridates
9. Library
10. Hill Houses
11. Tomb of Arsinoe
12. Curetes Street
13. Memmius Monument
14. Polio Fountain
15. Upper Agora
16. Prytaneon
17. Bouleuterion (small theatre)
18. Varius Baths

Characters

Agrippa	Roman General. Friend to Octavian
Amunet	Handmaiden to Princess Arsinoe
Antony	Consul of Rome. Triumvir
Arsinoe IV	Princess of Egypt
Atia	Mother of Octavian
Caesar, Julius	Roman Consul. Dictator of Rome
Caesarion	Son of Cleopatra VII of Egypt and Julius Caesar
Charmian	Handmaiden to Cleopatra
Claudius	Roman soldier, Ephesus
Cleopatra VII	Queen of Egypt
Cornelia	Julia's mother
Gaius	Julia's husband. Sculptor
Jacob	Paint shop owner, Sardis
Julia	Wife to Gaius
Korai	Handmaiden of Temple of Artemis, Ephesus
Lepidus	Roman General. Triumvir
Livia	Wife of Sextus. Friend to Gaius and Julia
Lucius Verres	Gaius' Patron, Ephesus
Marcus	Roman soldier, Ephesus
Megabyzus	High Priest, Temple of Artemis, Ephesus
Octavian	Later known as Augustus. Emperor of Rome
Petronius	First husband of Cornelia. Julia's father
Praxus	Second husband of Cornelia. Julia's stepfather

Publius	Library assistant, Ephesus
Quintus	Aide to Marcus Agrippa
Rufus	Roman soldier, Carcer Prison, Rome
Sargon	Slave and prostitute trader
Senior Senator	Official of Ephesus
Servilia	Sister of Livia
Sextus	Husband of Livia. Friend of Gaius and Julia
Suetonius	Assassin. Ex Roman legionary
Valerius	Roman Centurion, Ephesus

Part I

'A person's life is dyed with the colour of his imagination.'

Marc Antony

PROLOGUE

EGYPT

Outside Alexandria

Tabusiris Magna Temple

47BC

DARK WATER LAPPED at the boat as Amunet shivered in the cool desert night. She clutched the casket she was holding to her tightly. Slowly the boatman drew up to the lake's edge.

'Amunet, we can still go back, we can go to Thebes where no one will find us and take the casket with us,' he whispered.

'I gave my promise before the shrine in the temple of Hathor,' she replied. 'I cannot break my vow.'

The temple of Tabusiris Magna loomed ahead, appearing like a monstrous scarab beetle squatting on the deserted desert sands.

'Be quick then, we must leave this place.'

Her companion pulled the boat up onto the sand and she stepped ashore, the murky water leaving a jagged stain along the hem of her robe. It was unlikely she would encounter Roman soldiers here, but still she moved carefully and quietly looking for any sign of movement around the outside of the temple.

Reaching the outer pylon she walked through into the inner courtyard. Inscrutable statues of Horus stared down at her as she glided into the inner entry. With relief she saw the portly figure of the High Priest moving towards her a warning finger to his lips.

'My lady asks that this casket be given to you for safekeeping as was agreed,' whispered Amunet.

The priest led her down underneath the temple to the tunnels below. Seldom entered and dimly lit by oil lamps, they smelled of moist earth and age. Entering one of the last of the underground cells she followed him to a small wall niche.

'I will hold the casket under my protection as promised,' the aged priest said softly. 'Go in safety with the blessing of Horus.'

CHAPTER 1

ROME
Caesar's Egyptian Triumph
46BC

THEY MUST NOT smell her fear!

Arsinoe prayed to Isis for courage as the long stretch of the Via Sacra swung into view. Sweat dripped down her face stinging her eyes and momentarily blinding her. Already she had walked, exhausted, fighting the weight of her heavy chains from the Campus Martius, around the Circus Maximus and, finally, the Palatine Hill.

As she gazed down past the temple of Castor and Pollux she saw row upon row of marble temples and buildings, a display of Rome's awesome wealth and unyielding power. The cacophony of noise was unending as the leering, unwashed rabble pressed in upon her. Already the musicians and dancers with their drums and sistrums wound their way into the Forum followed by gold, gold, and more golden items of every description, ripped from the palace and temples of her beloved Alexandria.

Caged crocodiles, hippopotami and panthers drew gasps of awe from the exultant crowd as they trundled past. On and on rolled the procession as huge, oversized statues appeared. Next came the massive group of dirty, bedraggled Egyptian slaves. Among them Arsinoe could see her eunuch tutor, Ganymedes. He could be little use to her now, or even to himself. A miniature replica of the Alexandrian Pharos Lighthouse lumbered behind her, flames spewing from its summit.

So this was mighty Rome! At least they had bathed and dressed her according to her rank the more to add to Caesar's glory as she preceded his chariot. She was the ultimate prize, an Egyptian princess dragged through the dust and the jeers. Finally she saw her sister surrounded by the white clad senators and Caesar's family.

She held her head high. I am true Pharaoh of Egypt – and my ugly, jealous sister, how much you want me dead! Cleopatra the whore! Cleopatra who has sold her body to the Romans to keep for herself the crown of Egypt! A murderer who has killed her brother, Ptolemy, and now watches this spectacle as if she were one of them, in this Triumph over the land of Amun.

The chains bit into her wrists as she was jerked to a sudden halt. Caesar descended his chariot and walked to the victory dais. For a brief few moments the crowd stilled. Then a great roar began and swelled until it reached a crescendo.

Arsinoe knew her time had come. The Tullianum prison strangler awaited her. At least she would meet her end away from gloating Roman eyes. Hatred filled her whole being for these uncouth Romans, but most of all for her ambitious, power mongering sister.

A great calmness settled over her. She would die with dignity. Her striking, raven black hair hung down to her shoulders, she turned her beautiful face and her dark eyes sought Cleopatra's one last time. The look was one of utter loathing.

At that moment, frozen in time, Arsinoe looked exactly what she was. Despite the chains, dirt and humiliation, she was an Egyptian princess and the last of the pure Ptolemy bloodline!

Chapter 2

TURKEY
Ephesus
46BC

A teeming mass of goods, people and animals vied with each other at the harbour for the business of the city of Ephesus. One of the busiest commercial ports of the Roman world, lying at the mouth of the Cayster River where it flowed into the Aegean Sea, it provided shelter to many vessels some, by necessity, anchored offshore awaiting entry.

The docks area was only for the loading and unloading of military and commercial goods, with shops located in or closer to the city itself. Merchants took delivery of purchases ordered from the rest of the Roman world, of a diversity and quality to gladden the hearts of the city's inhabitants.

Spices, incense, and rich materials as well as other handicrafts filled the ships' holds. Wines, olive oil and other agricultural products were produced locally, but many other items were purchased from the rich offerings available elsewhere.

Glass from Egypt, prized for its beauty, especially perfume bottles, sold quickly in Ephesus, as well as ivory goods, silks from China and huge amphorae filled with a higher quality olive oil from the desert areas around Bahariya, Egypt. The amphorae, made there and filled with the precious liquid, were carried on long journeys by camels over the shifting desert dunes. They were then transported on to the Empire's many, far flung destinations.

The strongest commercial link was with Egypt's major trading partner, Alexandria, which supplied wheat as well as other luxuries. Thus, the volume of trade passing through the port was such as to make many a local merchant very wealthy and able to enjoy the very best life had to offer.

On this particular day, under the blue skies and summer heat typical of Ephesus, the 200,000 inhabitants of the city saw no reason to do other than go about their business as they did on any other day. There was nothing out of the ordinary except, perhaps, for the reading of animal entrails by the temple priest which predicted uncertain times ahead. Still, he mused, everything seemed peaceful enough.

One of those seeking to slip unnoticed through the harbour throng was a young woman of Egyptian appearance. Tall, with long brown hair and a face and figure admired with many a lustful glance, her dark eyes searched anxiously out to sea. Apparently satisfied, Amunet retreated to a stone bench to watch and wait.

Barely had she moved, when a covered litter was carried in haste to the shaded area under the trees by four heavily muscled slaves and set down under the nearest tree. The occupant, a small, thin man elaborately dressed and wearing expensive rings and jewellery emerged. As Amunet had done, he gazed expectantly towards the sea, then also settled down to wait.

Neither had to wait long. A Roman quinquereme carrying soldiers and slaves entered port and prepared to unload its cargo. Prefect Marcus Claudius glared as he began to supervise the unloading. Merchants and slaves had managed to cover the area now in front of the quinquereme with their own dolia and amphorae.

'Move it! Get those out of my sight or I'll confiscate them and you can join the slaves headed for the slave market!' He roared. A frenzy of movement followed as merchants removed the offending goods.

The occupant of the litter had strolled down to the scene and was now standing directly in front of the gangplank watching the first of the soldiers disembarking.

'You, you little turd! Stay out of my way Sargon! You'll no doubt be delighted to know there are plenty of sound slaves on board for you to get your grimy hands on. Just make sure you pay your taxes!'

'Whatever you say!' Sargon sneered.

Marcus turned away. He felt sick to his stomach every time he laid eyes on the man. Well known as the principal slave and prostitute trader in Ephesus, and one of its richest citizens, Sargon was also despised for his corruption, cruelty and perversions.

The slaves, men, women and children of all ages male and female were herded down onto the docks and escorted up Arcadian Street to the city. A long walk of some 530 metres, on a road built of stone slabs, it was physically difficult for the sick, young and old and nearly always the start of an often miserable life.

Back on board, Marcus had only one duty remaining. Selecting ten of his most trustworthy soldiers he ordered a thin, young woman into marching place between them. Her body was filthy and her long, black hair hung matted and uncombed to her shoulders.

'Guard her well, and mark you deliver her only to the High Priest.' Marcus ordered.

'If you fail, you will answer to Caesar himself!'

With that, they marched through the docks and disappeared up Arcadian Street.

Amunet's eyes filled with tears. At the last moment, in the shadow of the prison strangler, Caesar had spared Arsinoe's life. Her punishment was lifelong exile in the city of Ephesus.

Chapter 3

JULIA WAS BEAUTIFUL. She often wore her long blond hair back in a bun. The pale, flawless skin of a face with small, perfect features and cute dimples, accentuated exquisite green eyes. A little more than of average height, her slim but feminine figure drew many an admiring glance.

Right now, however, she was engaged in the rather unglamorous chore of cleaning the small home in which she lived with her new husband, Gaius. She was much admired as a young Roman woman considered highly marriageable and from a very respectable if not patrician family. She was as virtuous and sensible as she was beautiful. Rejecting several offers of marriage, she waited for the special man who would win her heart.

Julia had known, of course, the minute she had laid eyes on Gaius. Tall, with dark hair, he was lean of build with an air of confidence, and a spontaneous smile. A talented sculptor and stone mason, he shared with her an interest in culture.

As for Gaius, he loved the soft innocence about her that made Julia seem so vulnerable. With her pale skin and golden hair she seemed to glow like a ray of sunshine. She had a look of 'class' about her but was also blessed with a sense of fun, and he knew he would love her forever.

Many thought that with her beauty she should have married a man of wealth rather than a poor sculptor, but what she wanted was a man who would love her while sharing her interests, and with whom she felt a special physical chemistry.

As her family had little wealth, she had learned early that although enough money for reasonably comfortable survival was necessary, and to be welcomed, there were other qualities far more important for true personal happiness.

Soon after they married, Gaius was offered and accepted, a commission from a rich Ephesian patron which provided them with a home, excellent remuneration and the type of work he most enjoyed. And so they set up their new home in Ephesus.

Julia's thoughts were interrupted as Gaius came through the door. 'I simply can't get the right marble, Julia. It's just not possible to sculpt something beautiful from marble with flaws!' He sighed and slumped onto the nearest bench.

The marble came from a nearby quarry and as he refused to sculpt anything he considered less than perfect, he often found himself having to waste precious time going to the quarry to select suitable marble blocks himself.

'How am I ever to finish my commissions for the Artemisium on time if I can't get the right marble, or I spend all my time travelling?' Gaius looked thoroughly miserable.

Julia was used to his despondency when he was less than satisfied with his work. Taking his face gently in her hands she kissed him tenderly and drew him to his feet.

'Oh Gaius, the right marble will come, you'll see! The goddess will wait a little longer.'

He kissed her deeply while untying her hair sending it tumbling onto her shoulders, then led her to their sleeping chamber. Love wove its magic in the intensity of their passion.

The evening meal was late that night.

—

Flanked by her guards, Arsinoe was marched up Arcadian Street eventually reaching the large, square, commercial Agora on the right hand side at the starting point of the inner city. The shops sold all manner of goods and the air was filled with bartering and the noise of heatedly conducted business transactions.

After the sea voyage the smell of spices and food cooking made her feel nauseous. She noted people of many races from fair, long haired Gauls to dark haired Greeks and exotic looking Persians as well as the soldiers and ragged beggars who frequented every large Roman city.

In front of her on the side of a hill a huge theatre rose up, its marble lined seats gleaming impressively in the sun. It marked the start of Marble Street, the beginning of the Royal Road the main section of which ran from the elegant city of Sardis to Susa, Persia. Statues, marble paving stones and restful gardens with fountains beautified Marble Street.

The Great Theatre dominated Ephesus, and not just because of its size. The Theatre was the hub of gladiatorial, literary and musical events. Huge by the standards of any city in the Empire, this venue unashamedly proclaimed Ephesus' wealth and influence. The three storied stage area stood eighteen metres high, its facade decorated with marble statues in niches, as well as columns and reliefs. Multiple doors, the central one wider than the others, opened to the orchestra area. The Theatre stood as a stunning example of quality workmanship, which continued here to this time.

No one paid much attention to Arsinoe except for the occasional curious glance. The passage of slaves, pilgrims or soldiers through Ephesus was expected and unremarkable. She saw around her a rich, beautiful city with an impressive library, and on the hillside, rows of terrace houses with red tiled roofs. In the distance stood a lovely little temple in the Egyptian style dedicated to Serapis. Although nothing could ever match her beloved Alexandria, nonetheless, she was impressed.

A sharp turn took them up steep Curetes Street. They had not gone far when Arsinoe felt a sudden, unexplained chill of fear, but it passed as quickly as it had come. On they walked past the Upper State Agora with its Temple to Isis, and surrounded by other buildings and monuments and the Prytaneion or Town Hall, including an assembly hall, administration rooms and the State Archives.

Arsinoe glanced across at a perpetual flame sacred to Vesta which was kept burning day and night by the city's elite families. She was escorted further for more than a mile after they were outside the ancient city walls. Finally they reached their destination. It took her breath away.

Built on land that had been a swamp, the imposing Temple of Artemis stood 377 feet in length and 180 feet wide, consisting of 127 Ionic style columns each 60 feet high. The exterior was classical in style, built entirely of marble and stood on three raised levels with marble steps.

Arsinoe was surprised at the quality of the columns which were carved with intricate reliefs obviously crafted by a skilled artisan. Many were decorated with delicate touches of colour and gilding that glinted in the sunlight. Above the steps leading into the interior stood an impressive, deep pronaos with several pairs of columns within it, inviting pilgrims to enter. The sea voyage to Ephesus had been long and unsettling. She was exhausted and longing for the comfort and safety she hoped to find inside.

Although the land was naturally marshy, extensive efforts had been made to cultivate grassed areas, which served as gardens and displayed formal, exquisite statues, providing graceful additions to the already elegant structure. Arsinoe glimpsed a tantalising hint of blue water in the distance. Most surprising, however, were the musicians and colourful dancers and acrobats performing near the front steps of the magnificent Temple, as she approached.

It was the only structure she had ever seen which rivalled the Pyramids and temples of Egypt in both size and splendour. The Temple was well known as a refuge for rich political refugees.

'Halt! Stand Down!'

At the Centurion's command, the soldiers stopped at the base of the broad marble steps as an aged man dressed in the robes of the Megabyzus, the High Priest, came down the steps towards her.

'You are welcome Queen Arsinoe, please enter and we will see to your comfort.' With a nod of dismissal to the military escort, he led her inside. She had reached the only place where she was safe from an execution order which had just been issued against her from Alexandria, Egypt.

Chapter 4

45BC

SARGON WAS HAVING a good day! His latest batch of slaves had arrived at the market in surprisingly fit condition due to luck and fair weather sailing. He had sold an aged but educated Gaul as a family tutor at a good price and three young girls were bought by families as maids. He had also made a particularly good profit from one of his best customers, who had been looking for gardening and house slaves and had been pleased with several young, strong, male Egyptians.

'You must come to us one evening to dine.' Sargon's elite client waved his hand airily.

'I would be delighted to accept.' Sargon glowed with pleasure.

The world was looking decidedly rosy. He allowed himself to savour the thought of the enjoyment to come later from the nubile body of Leila, his favourite prostitute. He really must expand that side of his business, he thought. Demand seemed to be ever increasing, and the three establishments he owned were pushed to their limits to provide service to so many customers.

Sargon's favourite and most upmarket establishment stood at the junction of Marble and Curetes Streets. Inside was a large, square foyer with a relaxing central fountain in the shape of Venus, and reclining couches where refreshments were served to clients. Ten private cubicles lined the foyer perimeter. For important groups of clients, musicians were also often provided. The establishment's services were expensive, as the women who worked here were exclusive. They were very experienced and willing to meet the most 'unique' needs of rich and famous customers. Each girl had her own 'speciality' and this was pictured above her cubicle. Highly suggestive frescoes adorned the inner walls and a stone bed provided the only necessary furniture.

Sargon was somewhat annoyed at an official sign that had recently been posted up on the wall near the Mithridates Gate proclaiming '*Do Not Piss Here'* as he felt that it lowered the 'tone' of the area. Nonetheless, he considered his establishment the very best in Ephesus. The money kept rolling in.

Recently he had tried a new form of advertising which had proved to be a master stroke as it had increased his business many times over. In Marble Street and in several other locations, he had arranged for marble paving stones with the imprint of a foot and a picture of one of his prostitutes to replace the existing street paving stones. The new ones indicated the direction of his 'pleasure' establishments.

He had arrived in Ephesus three years before. A Syrian by birth, his father had kicked him out of home at an early age. A young Sargon had used his street knowledge and natural intelligence to survive. Now in his late twenties, he had a record of thuggery and assassinations. Not that he got his own hands bloody. His money ensured that he was never directly implicated.

The colonnaded terrace house he owned was in a much desired central location. It was comfortably furnished, had hot and cold running water, and was decorated with brightly coloured frescoes on the walls.

Although there were no windows, the doorway allowed the sun to stream in, dispelling the gloom. The interior was large and included a vestibule, impluvium, two sitting rooms, a dining room, kitchen and toilet. There was also a most pleasant, shaded peristyle courtyard, where one could sit and relax.

Sargon entered the brothel before opening time, noting admiringly the pretty fountain with its gently cascading water, the musicians preparing their instruments and the slaves laying out the presentation of pastries and wine on the side tables. His eyes went to the prostitutes standing to one side, in a group. Searchingly his eyes lingered over their scantily clad bodies, mentally caressing exposed breasts. He altered the position of a couple of couches, then clapped his hands. They gathered around him.

'Ladies!' His smile, meant to be charming, made him look more like an oily ferret than usual. 'I pay you very well to provide quality services to my clients. Remember, they come here to get what they can only demand at home. They desire your bodies, but most of all they want the illusion of love and passion. Here, they will get as much of that as they pay for. If a client requests something a little "special," give it to him. Above all, you must always respond with enthusiasm. Our clients will be here very soon. Make yourselves ready!'

Perhaps, thought Sargon, he would even find time later today to attend the theatre where gladiatorial contests were being held.

Life was good!

—

EPHESUS – THEATRUM MAXIMUS

Games Program

Procession of Exotic Animals

Praegenarii – The Clowns

In The Afternoon

Gladiatores

Thracian V Hoplomachi

Provocateur V Samnite

Secutor V Retiarius

On the hill of Panayir the 24,000 seat Theatre was filling fast with a noisy, happy crowd looking forward to an exciting afternoon's entertainment.

The usual merchandise was selling well at the small stalls near the entrance which specialised in items such as children's toys, small gladiator statues and oil lamps. Food was also available and popular with those who had come straight to the Theatre from work or other activities.

Gaius and Julia had decided to treat themselves to a day of leisure in the company of friends Sextus and Livia. The two couples had become close after meeting when Sextus became an assistant sculptor to Gaius, and they worked together on most days. Their taste in entertainment was similar and the two women always enjoyed shopping together.

Time away from work was a luxury for both men who struggled to cope with an ever increasing volume of work, resulting from a need for more construction, both homes and buildings, and restoration works at the Artemisium and other public monuments. The population of Ephesus continued to increase as the city's reputation spread for beauty, culture, good weather and as a safe harbour.

The couples had met earlier in the day for a good natured game of backgammon then a rest at the Pollio Fountain.

'I wouldn't mind a few more days off to relax like this,' smiled Sextus.

'You'd be so bored after a while you wouldn't know what to do with yourself,' Gaius teased.

Livia swirled the water with her fingers enjoying the cool sensation and the mist coming off the fountain's water in the slight breeze.

'If either of you two have too much time on your hands, Julia and I could always do with some more help around the house you know!'

Both women laughed and Livia ruffled Sextus' wavy brown hair with her hand. 'You're lucky to be off work, so make the most of it!'

Sextus, relaxed by nature and quiet was well matched with the more bubbly Livia. She was short in stature with straight light brown hair, and a rounded, pleasant and 'open' face which showed her emotions. They were a happy couple and enjoyed life. Julia thought it would probably not be long before they had a child. They would, she thought, make good parents.

It was a warm day with the threat of a late afternoon thunder storm. The crowd was noisily betting on their favourites while a small group of musicians played. This was followed by the Bestiarii leading out the animal parade which began the program, followed by the Praegenarii, - clowns fighting with wooden weapons purely for comic effect, while latecomers took their seats.

The clowns entered tumbling and smiling to the applause of the spectators. The sound of cymbals clashing and trumpets blaring signalled their arrival, accompanied by gasps of admiration at their athleticism and colourful costumes. 'Ave! Ave!' They called a greeting to the crowd. A couple of pairs dressed as gladiators, carrying ridiculously oversized shields, immediately set to fighting each other with blunt swords far smaller than the real thing, while the remaining clowns performed cartwheels and tricks. The spectators joined in the make believe, mocking them with good humour, and demanding they kill one other, while knowing that for these performers, it was an impossibility.

'Morituri Te Salutant'

The main action of the day centred around three later gladiatorial bouts. The third proved the most popular. The gladiators saluted the crowd in the traditional way. This was a bout between a Secutor wearing a helmet with round eye holes carrying a shield and gladius, and wearing an arm protector and a greave on one leg, and a Retiarius.

Although having no head or face covering, the Retiarius carried a small dagger, had an arm protector and used a net with which to entangle his opponent. Both fought bare footed. The bout was evenly matched between two experienced gladiators and thoroughly enjoyed by the noisy, totally captivated crowd.

Despite some of the more bloodthirsty amongst them yelling, Lugula! *Lugula!—Run him through!*—whenever they sensed the Secutor gaining an advantage,—most were satisfied when the bout finally ended in a draw. No gladiators would have graves dug for their bodies in the gladiators' cemetery today. They left the arena waving to the crowd, amidst much enthusiastic cheering. The ominous, black, waterlogged clouds, sent by angry gods, finally released their burden, as the threatened thunderstorm broke over the waiting city.

Torrents of rain pelted down and fierce lightening sent the crowd running for the exits. The citizens of Ephesus could never have foreseen that this day's thunderstorm was merely a mild hint of the chaos to come, from an event which would send their city and the rest of the Roman world into a bloodbath.

Chapter 5

ROME
Caesar's Villa Outside The Walls
45BC

A cascading rainbow of coloured fragments seemed to float in slow motion to the floor as the vase shattered against the wall. For a few moments time stopped, then lurched forward with the sound of Cleopatra's screeching.

'He called her what?' Cleopatra raged.

'Did you say he welcomed her as Queen?'

The shaking messenger barely managed to squeak an answer. 'Yes, your majesty, the Megabyzus welcomed her to the Temple using that title.'

Cleopatra was rigid with fury. 'Charmian!' she shrieked, 'Charmian!' Her maid hurried into the room.

'Have this mess cleaned up and keep Caesarion away from it!'

'Yes, Majesty,' she replied and fled.

They were living in an opulent villa belonging to Caesar which lay just outside the walls of Rome. This arrangement provided some small mask of respectability for Caesar's wife, Calpurnia, and also gave as little ammunition as possible to Caesar's opponents in the Senate. In reality, as a foreign ruler, Cleopatra was forbidden by law to live inside the walls of Rome.

She turned to the messenger who had now fallen to his knees.

'Convey my extreme displeasure to the High Priest and tell him that Arsinoe is NOT the Queen of Egypt, and she is under order of execution for treason. As for the rest of you, you must watch her even more closely. Now, leave me!'

The messenger backed out of the room as low and as quickly as possible.

Cleopatra had placed spies in Ephesus as a precaution, to watch Arsinoe and they had kept her informed from the time she had arrived at Arcadian Street. Cleopatra was in no doubt that her sister would plot against her in another power play. Why, oh why, hadn't Caesar just let the prison executioner squeeze the life from Arsinoe's pretty little throat when they had the opportunity?

She wandered outside into the stillness of the lush, green garden. The Roman sun was setting over the high villa walls, and she could hear the gurgling of the water gently cascading from the central font of the water fountain. Settling herself on the outside of its surrounds, she sat quietly running her fingers along the rough texture of the stone. Finally, allowing her body to relax, little by little her anger subsided.

In its place, from deep down in the very core of her being was reasserted her determination that Caesarion, her son and Caesar's, must one day rule both Egypt and Rome. That was his destiny! Nothing or no one must ever be allowed to interfere. She stood and quietly walked through to her writing table inside, the hem of her gown whispering over the marble floors.

After Caesar's pardon, Cleopatra herself had proclaimed an execution order against her half sister issued from Alexandria, but there was no way of carrying it out while Arsinoe remained within the sanctuary of the Temple of Artemis. The tradition of refuge could not be violated. Or could it? Cleopatra sat down to plot the end of her one remaining rival for Egypt's throne. Arsinoe had proven a formidable foe in the Battle of Alexandria, even against Caesar. One way or another, she would die!

The next morning having taken what she considered suitable measures to ensure Arsinoe's silence, even though she would have to wait some time to put her plan into action, Cleopatra, having grown tired of being in the restrictive space inside the villa, - decided to go shopping.

'Charmian, we will leave Caesarion in the care of Iras and the other servants here and you and I will visit the Forum and the shops. Call for the litter!'

Heavily veiled, and with the litter privacy curtains drawn, Cleopatra settled back to enjoy a morning of bartering and buying before the Forum became too busy. There were shops elsewhere, however, she enjoyed visiting the most exclusive of them which were located in the Basilica Aemilia.

Veiled as she was and conservatively dressed, it was possible for her to move around the Forum without raising curious stares or being recognised. Four aisles in a marble hall in the Basilica Aemilia catered for the needs of the most discerning of buyers.

'Would you like some scent today for yourself?' Cleopatra enquired of Charmian.

'Yes, my Lady. You are most kind. What are you looking to buy?'

Cleopatra smiled. 'I rather fancy some scented oils for when Caesar visits next, as well as perfumed bath water. I think either the lemon or frankincense, although I hear the orange is heavenly. Maybe I may even try the ointment recommended to me by Antony's wife, Fulvia, at dinner the other night. Apparently I have many fragrances to choose from such as myrrh or honey.'

Small shops lined the aisles. Usually they each consisted of only one room, at the most two, with a picture of their wares painted on the wall outside. Each shop faced directly onto the aisles and had front wooden shutters which were closed at night to stop the many thieves in the city making off with the merchandise.

As Rome had no police force, thievery was a constant problem for the shopkeepers. Cleopatra found one store which specialised in silks. Luxuriating in the feel of the soft, lustrous cloth, she marvelled at the brilliant colours and bought a role of material exactly matching her memory of the deep blue of the Nile.

After an enjoyable morning's shopping they returned to the villa, Cleopatra having totally cleared her mind of the problems and decisions of the day before. She expected that either that night or the next, she would have need of the oils and perfumed bath water to prepare for Caesar's next visit.

It was, in fact, several days before Caesar visited her. He was having trouble with the faction in the Senate which consistently tried to thwart his will. Caesar's 'love-hate' relationship with the old Senator, Cicero was alive and well.

Caesar admired his intellect and huge powers of oratory, but the honey tongued veteran clashed constantly with him in matters of policy, not to mention the pamphlets he insisted on continuing to write which were widely circulated especially while Caesar had been away. Cicero, however, was the least of his concerns.

Trying to force through land reforms, Caesar was also constantly debating with the likes of Cassius, Trebonius and Casca. The Senate House became the scene of verbal slanging matches with much jeering and abuse heard in the chamber. His dalliance with Cleopatra in Egypt had been ammunition for his enemies, but now with her actually living virtually in Rome, there was talk in the Senate of interference by foreigners in Roman politics.

Known in the past for his affairs with married women, a 'blind eye' had generally been turned to his ex marital 'arrangements' but these were women who, although married, were at least, usually Roman.

As with Cleopatra, however, he did have a weakness for affairs with Queens from foreign lands, including Eunoe, a moor who was a married woman. Most scandalous by far was his alleged affair with King Nicomedes of Bithynia which became a joke and the subject of many earthy marching songs of banter, openly sung by his soldiers. Cicero declared scathingly in the Senate - 'No more of that, pray, for it is well known what he gave you, and what you gave him in turn.' Their relationship, understandably, turned even more icy.

It was well known that he had an ex marital relationship with Servilia, mother of Brutus, who was even rumoured to be his son. Caesar was now increasingly being spoken of by some as having become arrogant of the will of the Senate. For many, the accusations were frivolous and sprang from jealousy. However, the friction was increasing.

Although concerned, Caesar had decided that he needed to conduct a campaign in Parthia. The timing was not ideal with so much unrest around, but he felt he could not wait much longer. Parthia was always a danger to Rome, and he intended to put an end to the problem once and for all. He decided to leave around the middle of March of next year unless something occurred too important to ignore. He was sure that Antony was more than capable of handling things in Rome should the need arise.

Tired and starting to feel his increasing years and ever more frequent attacks of the falling sickness, Caesar finally made his way one late afternoon to his Egyptian mistress, waiting for him at the villa.

The drizzling rain suited his mood and it was with heavy steps that he entered. His young son, Caesarion, was the first to see his father and, tearing towards the door, flung himself into Caesar's arms.

The child was a constant source of joy to both of his parents, his happy nature providing some respite from the conflicts around him.

'How's my favourite Centurion? Have you been practising your Latin today?' enquired Caesar, laughing.

This, then, he thought, is the reason for everything. The reason for living from day to day and, hopefully, year to year. This is enough to give purpose to life!

Cleopatra watched them silently from the doorway. That Caesar adored his young son was obvious. She wished that he did not have to leave Rome so soon, as the next few months until he left, would pass quickly, she knew. Still, as a ruler herself, she understood and accepted that he must do what he felt necessary both as a duty to Rome and for his own political survival.

She smiled up at him as she quietly entered the room. 'It's wonderful to see you. I'm so glad you came!'

For several moments there was silence, as his eyes searched her face. 'I'm sorry I have not been able to come before this, but Rome exhausts my time and energy,' he said seriously. 'Perhaps I should not have expected you to remain here instead of in Egypt. I understand it isn't easy for you, but I hope you know that there is nowhere I would rather be, than with you. I am tired beyond belief, but when I'm here, the burden is lighter.'

The night which followed was a gentle one. Perfumed scents from the bathwater, oils and ointments wafted through the air as Cleopatra welcomed Caesar's body and soothed his mind. He allowed himself to totally relax with her in a way he could not with any other. Initially hard on this evening to arouse, his natural physical attraction to her, which had always been strong, overcame the worries and tiredness and finally he found release.

Chapter 6

EPHESUS
45BC

Gliding gently in a softly swaying boat on the Nile she could smell the heady, slightly cloying perfume of the lotus flower, favoured by Egypt's Queens and her peace was total. Serenity enveloped her Ka.

Arsinoe opened her eyes only to find with regret that her dream was broken and she lay in her room in the Temple. Her stay there so far had been pleasant, her days taken up with prayer at the small shrine to Isis, visits from the faithful Amunet, her chief lady in waiting, and writing to those friends and supporters still loyal to her as true Queen of Egypt.

She sighed as she rose to bathe, dress and eat the first meal of the day. Amunet was due to arrive later with any information or gossip she had heard in the city or around the harbour. Arsinoe had quickly regained both her weight and her beauty after entering the Temple, but she grew restless and frustrated with her inability to influence her future and her enforced confinement.

She reflected upon her impressions of her new home. The Temple of Artemis was served by castrated priests and also by handmaidens known as Korai. Throngs of pilgrims from many countries visited the Temple.

The Goddess Artemis, known to the Romans as Diana, was revered as the Mother Goddess. Refered to in earlier times as Cybele, she was the patroness of Ephesus and much beloved by its citizens. She was also revered as the Goddess of Fertility but married women were excluded from entering the Temple on pain of death.

The Temple interior was airy, light and spacious with magnificent gilded decoration on its columns, and lion headed water spouts on the friezes. There were large public spaces and visitors' areas, and these overlooked gardens which were both beautiful and restful, while glimpses of blue water not far away caught the eye. The venerated wooden statue of Artemis in the inner shrine, featured multiple breasts with the Goddess depicted as wearing a mural crown and having her legs encased in a pillar.

Personally, Arsinoe found the statue repulsively ugly. By comparison she thought it lacking in the beauty and skill shown by Egyptian artisans, in their representations of Egyptian gods and goddesses. Arsinoe was homesick for Egypt's culture and the serenity of the ordered world of nature ruled over by the goddess Maat. On her return she would ensure that proper observance to preserve the true balance of order 'above as below' was even more strictly adhered to.

She walked through to the private garden at the rear of the Temple and stood gazing out at the shoreline in the distance. Memories of Alexandria flooded over her. Longingly she remembered the more pleasant moments of her childhood. Although conflict and deception was part of life for every member of the Royal Family she had often escaped to wander for long hours along the harbour front, looking out to sea.

Even in the palace the sound of the sea had never been far away and she loved its power as the waves crashed against the harbour walls. Unlike her half sister, Cleopatra, she had no love of learning, no yearning for books or to study languages. Arsinoe was a dreamer. Escaping in her imagination to other places and times, in her mind she lived varied lives, and gave her creativity free reign. She loved music and would sit for hours listening to the sistrums, flutes and drums of the court musicians. Arsinoe closed her eyes and as if down a long tunnel, her voice came pulsing back to her.

—

'Father, father, are we leaving yet? Where are you? Does Cleopatra have to come too?'

She saw herself running excitedly down the palace corridors, her maid desperately trying to keep up. Her father had come to her, laughing, and picking her up had whirled her round and round in the air before hugging her and placing her down on the nearest step.

'Arsinoe, my child, you must try to have patience we are leaving soon and it will be a long journey for you.'

Her father Ptolemy Auletes looked lovingly at his young daughter. It was important, he thought, that he enjoyed some personal time with his daughters, and he had decided that they alone, would accompany him on this trip.

Although young, Arsinoe's natural tendencies towards the mysteries and rites of the ancient Egyptian religious gods were already obvious and in keeping with her personality. Her creative and imaginative tendencies strengthened the attraction of priestly rituals and the sacred atmosphere of the temples.

That day they had begun a long journey to visit the Temple of Alexander the Great at the Bahariya oasis. They took with them Arsinoe's tutor, Ganymedes, a few attendants and a body of guards and horse handlers. Along the way they were met with rejoicing by the local villagers and given appropriate hospitality.

It seemed like only yesterday that she had seen the temple like a mirage through the shimmering heat as it rose from the desert dunes. The rays of the early morning sun struck the sandstone encasing the mudbrick walls, and she gazed in wonder. They stopped to appreciate the sight some distance away.

'Arsinoe,' whispered her father in her ear, 'this place is very special. A great leader called Alexander passed this way long ago, on his way from Siwa. This temple was built soon after as a dedication to him. Remember his name. When we return home I will take you to see him in the Soma.'

'Thank you, Papa, I would like that very much,' she said excitedly.

Continuing onwards they were greeted at the guard outposts as they passed through the southern access gate, and rode by the priests' houses. Met by the High Priest, they were invited into the dimly lit, cooler interior of the temple, to take part in a ceremony to Horus and Amun.

The smell of the incense and chanting of the priests was intoxicating as they faced the red granite altar. The intensity of the colour transfixed Arsinoe who could not draw her gaze away.

Later, on the temple walls, she looked upon the cartouche of Alexander. She also had memories of a magnificent relief. It showed him offering two vessels of wine to Horus and Isis. A ceremony was in progress with a priest, food offerings and incense.

Even the fascination of an excursion a couple of years later to the dual temple of Kom Ombo on the Nile, dedicated to the god, Sobek, with the crocodiles sunning themselves on the riverbank, lazing in the sun, failed to exceed her wonderment of that day at Bahariya. The crocodiles were loathsome, fearsome creatures, - the bringers of death, - to be treated with the respect due to the gods, and she determined to keep out of their reach.

'I am a crocodile immersed in dread, I am a crocodile who takes by robbery. I am the great and mighty fish like being who is in the Bitter Lakes.'

The Book of the Dead

Arsinoe's next experience soon after, was a visit to Djeseret, the 'Holy Place,' – the Valley of Deir el Bahari. The spectacular funerary temple of the Pharaoh Hatshepsut, lay in all its classic, pillared magnificence, in a valley surrounded by gigantic cliffs that reached forever for the sky. The building, facing west, had three ascending terraces with wide ramps leading to the highest levels. Arsinoe gazed at images of the land of Punt, showing a trading mission, and the incense trees, ebony, and baboons brought back to Thebes. The painted, limestone walls, gloried in the effect of varying shades of red, gold and bronze that dazzled the eye.

Something changed that day for Arsinoe! As she gazed upon the slim figure and into the small, serene face of the female Pharaoh on her throne, the realisation came to her, that female power was actually possible. Whether she wanted it, and at any cost, was another matter.

From that time onward she continued to worship at the magnificent main Serapeum Temple in Alexandria. Nonetheless, it was the Temple of Alexander which had left a lifetime impression.

The Serapeum Temple was dedicated to the god Serapis, a combination of Osiris, the god of the underworld, and Apis, the bull. Serapis was not a deity of the old traditional beliefs, but rather, a local god that emerged from Alexandria merging Greek and Egyptian tradition.

The Temple itself was magnificent with soaring, gilded pillars, a giant, thirty foot statue of the god, shrines to Osiris and Isis and magnificent decorations of gold and gems.

Worship of Serapis also flourished in Ephesus. There were strong links between Alexandria and Ephesus which had largely been built around trade, and a temple to Serapis as well as other facilities had been built in Ephesus to serve the needs of Egyptian merchants.

Colours used in Egyptian temples had specific meanings and were assigned to specific gods. Blue was associated with Amen-ra and the concept of resurrection, while white was the colour of death and the death shroud. Red signified the eye of Ra and indicated the most powerful of the gods. It was the colour gold, however, which had a variety of meanings. It could indicate the plentiful nature of the harvest or the return of one's spirit to an all powerful god.

Magic and mystery were also an integral part of Egyptian religion. *'Not only was the practice of magic well established in dynastic Egypt, but it was a fundamental part of the religion.'*

'The Arcadian Cipher.'

Arsinoe loved the Royal Palace. With its huge throne room and bathing and reception areas it oozed luxury. Wide, gleaming, marble steps ascended or descended from sweeping, luxurious, marble floors, defining specific rooms. Generous openings and views to the gardens and harbour, lent airiness and light. Bathing pools adorned with blue and pink lotus blossoms added exotic perfume and colours. The sound of the sea could be heard in the blue waters of the nearby harbour, sometimes tranquil, at others, thundering. Statues adorned corners and exits to gardens, and the music of flutes added a haunting, almost fleeting, unreal effect.

She especially loved her own room. It looked out over the gardens and the harbour and was spacious and light. She had always been intoxicated by the perfume of the lotus flower, the perfume of Egypt's Queens, and the smell of the blossom gently lingered in her room.

The filmy white curtains that covered her window picked up the most gentle of breezes, dancing as if in time to the breath of the gods. She had her own personal maid and tutor, and life was pleasant for the young princess except for 'spats' with her own family.

She would sneak a peek at foreign visiting ambassadors as her father sat in the throne room receiving them. One day, she thought, she would need to be ready to perform such duties. As a princess of the royal family she would occasionally also be included in ceremonies which required the family to attend events outside the walls of the palace.

She thought the city of Alexandria was incredibly beautiful. She saw a city with two wide, major avenues crossing each other, Canopic Avenue and Royal Avenue. Canopic Avenue ran from the Moon Gate entry in the city walls, right through the city to the

Sun Gate at the other end, while Royal Avenue led to the Palace and gardens.

The city was set out on a grid pattern and had the usual large city requirements of an Agora, Law Courts, the Temple of Serapis, a Stadium, Theatre, Gymnasium and Necropolis. It had a very large Jewish population. Most renowned, however, was the Library of Alexandria. Holding half a million scrolls, it was the largest in the known world. The city had its poor quarters but also mansions of great wealth and beauty.

The Temple of Serapis, a local Deity, was particularly beloved by the ordinary people who attended the religious rites in large numbers. The most unique feature of the city, however, was Alexandria's fabulous lighthouse set on the Isle of Pharos. It welcomed visitors to Alexandria's shores and could be seen well out at sea.

As time went by, Ptolemy Auletes' behaviour became more and more erratic. Also a lover of music, he was sarcastically referred to by many as 'the flute player.' He thought nothing of playing with local Alexandrians in the Palace and would ask embarrassed officials –

'How was that?'

'Wonderful, Majesty.' Was the unsurprising reply.

As Arsinoe grew older and her beauty bloomed, she also became increasingly aware of Cleopatra's hostility at the compliments Arsinoe received. They were not full sisters and that was reflected in their physical appearance. The physical beauty belonged to Arsinoe – the intellectual capacity to Cleopatra.

Sighing, Arsinoe made her way back inside the Temple of Artemis. Already she had met a variety of political figures, some of whom had been refugees in the Temple for a number of years. She spoke a few words pleasantly to each of them but resolved not to enter into lengthy conversations. That way nothing she said could be used later against her. She would have to be very, very careful if she was to survive.

—

Everyday affairs went on much as usual in Ephesus, and a Senate meeting was presently in session that afternoon in the Bouleuterion in Curetes Street. The venue was a perfect little theatre with a half circular stage and a podium one meter higher than the orchestra. It could seat 1500 people, and as it also had a wooden roof, meetings or performances could be held there in all weather.

'The meeting will come to order!' declared the Senior Senator.

'The final matter we have before us today requiring a decision, concerns a complaint by a citizen about the notice which was placed on the wall beside the Gate of Mithridates. It warns those too lazy to seek the public latrines provided, against using the Gateway instead.

A request has been made to remove the notice.'

The Senate ruled in favour of retaining the notice and the meeting was declared closed.

In a performance that evening, the perfect little theatre brought something special to the Ephesians and the actors who performed there, – and that was a feeling of intimacy. Impossible to create in the larger theatre in Marble Street, this intimacy drew the small audience, including Livia and Sextus, into the fantasy world portrayed by the actors.

A visiting theatre group from Athens presented the tragedy, *Antigone* one of the greatest of Greek plays, written by the renowned playwright, Sophocles. Several actors together with a chorus, representing Theban elders brought the story to life as the audience watched on, entranced. The play began set in front of the Palace of Thebes. First the actors entered onstage then the chorus later, into the orchestra area.

Wearing elaborately designed masks made of wood or linen showing the expressions of the characters they represented, the actors gave inspired performances. Each changed the character they portrayed several times during the play.

Some masks were so well made they even indicated through the addition of beards, grey hair or other adornments, the ages of the characters. Livia thought the costumes were some of the best they had ever seen. Elaborate attention to detail added to the overall atmosphere, as did the presentation of the chorus of Theban Elders.

The number of deaths in the story left no doubt in the minds of the audience as to the tragic circumstances portrayed. In this play Antigone is one of the strongest representations of a female character in any play. She has courage, insight and determination in the face of an unbeatable and unenviable fate. Antigone foresaw and accepted her death:

'I knew that I must die

E'en hadst thou not proclaimed

It; and if death, is thereby

Hastened, I shall count it gain.'

Antigone

Much to Sextus' amusement Livia became quite emotional at Antigone's impending death and sniffled alongside him as the play neared its conclusion. The audience cheered and called the company of actors back for several encores before the evening finally came to an end, and they exited the theatre.

'What marvellous masks!' Livia said enthusiastically. 'It's been a wonderful evening, Sextus!'

'I really enjoyed it. Even with you sniffling beside me,' he teased, and was duly rewarded for his trouble with a good dig in the ribs.

Miles away in the foremost city of the Roman world were other men wearing masks of a different kind. Their murderous intentions were well hidden behind smiles and flattery, as they conspired and whispered in shadowy places.

Part II

'Because we focussed on the snake, we missed the Scorpion.'

Egyptian Proverb

CHAPTER 7

Caesar turned in his bed and muttered,
With a struggle for breath the lamp-flame guttered;
Calpurnia heard her husband moan:
"The house is falling,
The beaten men come into their own."

'The Rider At The Gate'
John Masefield

ROME
15TH March 44BC
The Ides of March

CINNA SHIELDED HIS eyes with his arm as the rain pelted down. A huge bird circled three times over the Senate House in the rain and howling wind, then flew high in the air headed for the Capena Gate, and out of Rome.

'I wonder what the augurs would make of that?' Cinna muttered to himself as he pulled his cloak more tightly around him.

'Nothing good, that's for sure!'

He was headed for the house of Cassius and the group of men who were gathering in the still inky blackness of the early hours of the day – plotting murder.

Giving the pre-arranged signal, he was admitted, the men already gathered, glancing up as he entered.

'I tell you we should have tried harder to get Antony! Then things would have gone a lot easier for us.' Casca complained.

'There is absolutely no way he would have joined us.' Brutus shook his head decisively.

'Why not?'

'Antony would not have seen it in his best interests. He loses nothing by not being a part of this attempt. But what if we fail? He stands to lose everything,' Brutus insisted. 'And we could not have trusted him!'

A flash of lightening lit up the room accompanied by a massive crash of thunder, further fraying the nerves of the conspirators.

'The *attempt* as you call it will NOT fail! Cassius yelled, thumping his fist on the table. 'Not if we all hold our nerve and we keep Antony out of the way.'

'I hear Caesar dismissed his Praetorian Guard escort a couple of days ago,' remarked Decius. 'Why would he be so careless?'

Cassius laughed grimly. 'Don't you know – He thinks he's divine! He's one of the gods now, so he thinks he's immortal! Its time we all made our way to our houses so we don't arouse any suspicion. We will all leave separately.'

The mounds of rubbish littering the city streets were blown up into the air and hurled along, whipping against any wall or person they came across. Each of the men left the house alone, walking with difficulty against the strength of the wind.

The homeless on this night huddled for whatever protection they could find in the porticos of the major buildings, some finding shelter for the price of a drink in an inn. Fallen trees or branches covered parts of the Palatine.

By sunrise the storm had blown itself out leaving a scene of destruction behind it. One of the statues in the garden adjoining the Temple of Vesta had fallen and shattered, sending the vestals to watch over the sacred flame, and the priests to warn all who passed by and would listen, of portents of danger from the gods. A watery sun struggled to rise as Rome's citizens came out of their houses to gawk at the damage.

During the night, Caesar's wife, Calpurnia, had woken screaming from her sleep, covered in sweat.

'Julius, something is very wrong. You must not go to the Senate today,' she cried.

'It's just a storm. I need to be there today. Can I allow my opponents to make comments that Caesar is afraid of a storm?'

Caesar laughed and put a calming arm around her shoulders. He decided to re-think his decision a little later, when word came from the augurs about ill omens having been seen around the city. He determined, however, that he would go when spoken to by some of the senators declaring their intentions of attending that day.

Assassination! The Forum Romanum was a living, seething mass of humanity. Perhaps the conspirators, those who had left Caesar's body bleeding at the foot of Pompey's statue in the great assembly hall, thought that this was their moment in history. But Rome is the people. And the people are Rome! Rome is the mob! They would make the judgement as to who would hold history in his hands.

On this day the world had been turned upside down. The city waited for just the suggestion of a spark to set off the tinderbox created by murderers who had fled the scene of their crime like cowards running from a battle. These were no heroes!

More than twenty conspirators led by Cassius and joined even by Caesar's loved friend Brutus declared that by killing Caesar, they had saved the Republic of Rome from the threat of Kingship. After all, had not Caesar just been declared 'Divus Iulius,' Julius the God, as well as Dictator of Rome for Life? Still, the people were by no means convinced.

> *'they saw his (Caesar's) body all bemangled with gashes of swords: then there was no order to keepe the multitude and common people quiet, but they plucked up formes, tables and stooles, and layed them all about the body, and setting them a fire, burnt the corse.,, they took the firebrands, and went unto their houses that had slaine Caesar, to set them a fire. Other also ranne up and downe the citie to see if they could meete with any of them, to cut them in peeces...'*
>
> Plutarch's *'Lives of the Noble Grecians and Romans.'*

Mark Antony became the man of the people. Friend to Caesar, famed for his oratory and holding the military power of Rome in his hands, Antony took his moment in history. Bearing no stain of conspiracy or murder, he joined with the people and faced down the conspirators. A born leader, his destiny changed forever in the space of a day.

The conspirators locked themselves away in the Temple of Jupiter Optimus Maximus, fearful of the wrath of the people, and for their very lives. Bickering amongst themselves they were now in a precarious position. Most of all they feared Antony and the power of the army.

Caesar's will, held by the Vestal Virgins, became all important as they waited to see if Antony would, as expected, become Caesar's heir as well as his avenging right arm. To make matters worse, it was later disclosed that Caesar had left some of his wealth to the people of Rome.

Antony, however, was not their only problem. Marcus Lepidus, a fervent follower of Caesar, as Master of the Horse, had been Caesar's deputy. A powerful and respected patrician, it was likely that he would come to terms with Antony in an alliance to militarily confront the conspirators.

Left with few options, Brutus and Cassius fled and gathered their forces in an all out struggle for survival. Rome braced for civil war.

Mark Antony, fearful for Caesarion, son of Caesar and Cleopatra, arranged for the urgent departure of Cleopatra and Caesarion back to Egypt. He knew the boy was not safe while Caesar's murderers were still free. As the Roman world learned mouth by mouth and country by country of the death of a god among men, it gasped at the sheer audacity of his murderers.

Cleopatra, devastated by Caesar's death returned to Egypt to bring up their son as the next Pharaoh. Antony was unaware as yet that a shadow was to fall across the path of his destiny and ultimately destroy him. Caesar's nephew, Octavian, young and with little life experience or military ability had been unexpectedly named Caesar's heir.

—

Atia didn't know whether to laugh or cry! Following the death of Caesar the news came of her son Octavian, having been named in his great uncle Caesar's will as his adopted son and heir. She was overjoyed for her son, but fearful for him as well.

She had been so protective of Octavian – had she done the right thing? Perhaps she should have loosened the reins more. Anyway, it was too late for that now! In her mind she saw her son, as if for the first time, as others might see him.

Slight of build and short of stature, he had the sort of looks that many would have called 'good looking', but in a feminine, delicate way. He had the sort of looks to make many a soldier snigger when they first met him, seeing him as anything but a soldier, and probably attracted to other men – a despised trait in the Roman army. Atia had either heard herself, or been told by friends of the comments of 'pansy' being aimed at Octavian behind his back.

Octavian had lost his birth father early in life. Although having an affectionate family relationship with Caesar, he had only served with him on a limited basis in Spain as a contubernalis, a sort of junior 'secretary.' A military man he was not! There had been no constant male in his life that he respected and who would 'toughen' him up. To make matters worse, his health had been a constant concern.

Octavian wheezed, coughed and spluttered his way through one asthma attack after another, with no real cure in sight. The attacks were worse in some places, and at particular times of the year. He also had a considerable number of spots over parts of his body. Atia sat down to write a message of congratulations but, of course, as always, one of concern to Octavian for his welfare.

Octavian with his friend Agrippa whom he had first met in Spain, were serving in Apollonia, when word came of Caesar's death, and Octavian's inheritance. He decided to return to Brundisium and thence to Rome.

'I am now Caesar!' he declared emphatically.

'And I will always consider you as such and stand by you.' Agrippa replied.

But Octavian had a problem! Either opposing him from now on, or in partnership with him, were two of the toughest, most experienced and powerful military men Rome had ever known, – Lepidus, and particularly Antony. On the positive side, Caesar himself had named Octavian as his heir, a discovery when announced by the Vestal Virgins who safeguarded wills, that must have been like a knife to the guts for the loyal Antony.

Having been temporarily absent, Antony arrived back in Rome himself to deal with Octavian, and in 43 BC an unlikely Triumvirate emerged, – Antony, Lepidus, Octavian.

With Brutus and Cassius having taken control of the East and with a large army backing them, Antony, Lepidus and Octavian raised their own army and went 'hunting.' Fate led them to a place called Philippi.

The countryside was marshy, the terrain, difficult. Brutus, catching Octavian's forces by surprise, attacked. Octavian hid not far away in the swamp. Cassius, not realising Brutus would be successful, died by his own hand. Antony's forces having then joined those of Octavian were successful in the second battle in October 42 BC. Brutus committed suicide. The pyres of burning soldiers lit the night sky of Philippi as Romans burned Romans, and the stench of the dead was terrible!

Antony, tired and battle stained, strode decisively into Octavian's command tent. Agrippa looked on.

'You can get up now!' Antony sneered down at him.

'I would have been there except for this wretched condition,' wheezed Octavian.

And so began a long battle for ultimate power between two giants of the Roman world of the future. That Antony had no respect for Octavian either as a soldier or a man was understandable. But what was it that Caesar had seen in him?

What Antony's observation and intuition did not tell him, was that behind Octavian's weak, sickly, unmilitary and even unmanly exterior, lay a deceptive and politically brilliant mind.

—

EPHESUS
Temple of Artemis

When news of Caesar's assassination reached Ephesus, Arsinoe sat on the stool at her table as Amunet brushed her shiny, dark hair. 'There is no hope! With Caesar dead I have lost his protection of my exile status guaranteeing my safety. My sister will find a way to kill me! Caesar could be cruel, but at least he respected justice and tradition. I can't be sure that the Temple will protect me. There is nowhere else that I can go without being found by Cleopatra.'

Although she was by nature tough and resilient, Arsinoe was feeling the pressure of her situation. Amunet had never seen her so upset. 'Isn't there anything that can be done my Lady? Surely the High Priest or someone else can protect you?'

Arsinoe sat frowning then rose and began pacing the floor. 'I am lost unless I can somehow make the first move. Amunet, perhaps it is nearly time to use the one item of bargaining power that I have left. If I am to survive I must have the protection of someone who has power.

I am sure that this Triumvirate will not last. Sooner or later there will be fighting amongst the three of them. I must choose one of them with whom to trade, and in doing so, negotiate both my freedom and my return as rightful Queen of Egypt. Which one to choose – that's the question? It should not be long before the situation resolves itself. Leave me now, for I have a great deal to think on.'

Arsinoe stared grimly at the scene outside her window. She had rarely felt so alone and unprotected as she did at this moment.

Amunet made her way through the temple and down the steps. She thought of that night in the desert outside Alexandria and of the precious item she had left with the priest of the Temple of Tabusiris Magna. Perhaps it would be enough to buy protection for her mistress, and even her return to power.

—

EGYPT
Alexandria
The Royal Palace

Cleopatra's return to Alexandria was greeted with a huge outpouring of joy from the people, who threw rose petals and flower garlands under her feet as she walked to the Palace. She thought to herself, it had been such a joy to see the unique Pharos Lighthouse come into view as her ship approached the coastline.

Cleopatra looked around her at this most beautiful of cities. Set on a jewel sea, Alexandria's palace and buildings displayed beauty and grace without the ugly over extravagance of Rome. Despite its many temples, she sensed Rome lacked the spirituality so evident here.

Her journey from Rome had been uneventful in terms of sailing conditions, but she had neither known nor cared. In her grief she seemed only to be able to see the senseless murder of Caesar as some punishment from the gods. Grieving, she was cared for by Charmian who watched over her as Cleopatra stared vacantly into space.

Once at the Royal Palace, her spirits lifted by the welcome she had received, Cleopatra allowed herself to simply settle back into her old routine and wander in the gardens, before calling her ministers to meet with her the next morning. They had faithfully cared for the country during her absence, but were relieved to have her make the decisions once more.

Her thanks were heartfelt and she rejoiced to see each of them again. Without Caesar, however, she told them, Rome would come after Egypt's gold and grain and attempt to subjugate her as it had its other colonies. They must use the wealth they were blessed with to build the best possible fleet of warships and strengthen the army. Strength was all Rome understood, and she was determined to meet them with as much as she could muster.

—

The Temple of Isis
Philae

> To come here is to let go of what it means to be only human and to enter into that part of us which glimpses eternity

Cleopatra realised she was exhausted, her body weak, her spirit grieving and her mind dulled. The time would soon come when she must fight for the survival not only of Egypt but of her son, Caesarion. She must be ready.

Ordering the Royal Barge to be prepared, she determined to recover with a journey on the Nile travelling as far as the Temple of Isis at Philae. There she would refresh her mind, body and spirit and seek the help of the goddess. Taking with her only Iras, Charmian and the necessary attendants she began her voyage of recovery.

'The Nile is unique,' she said as she lay back on her cushions.

'It has a serenity, a quietness that stills the mind and calms the spirit.'

Along the riverbank she saw her people going about their daily work, and knew that it was truly good to be home again. Day drifted into day and with each came tears of loss, the joy of memories and the beginning of a new, as yet very small spark of hope.

As always, the first sighting of the Temple, built of sandstone in 370 BC was achingly beautiful. It was set on an island located at the first cataract, with a background of brilliantly coloured flowers. To step onto its sacred ground was to enter a place with a feeling of deep spirituality.

'There are few such places in this world.' Cleopatra told Iras and Charmian.

'To come here is to let go of what it means to be only human and to enter into that part of us which glimpses eternity.'

The Temple of Isis was sacred to the goddess. Shown in human form with cow's horns and a sun disc, she was the wife of Osiris and mother of Horus, and the link between this world and the next. Worshipped throughout the land, she was especially, the goddess of protection.

Cleopatra, the 'daughter' of Isis, looked to the great goddess for her safety. Her need of that protection, was the central reason for Cleopatra's journey down the Nile to this particular Temple to Isis. It had received the prayers of numerous pilgrims since ancient times.

The Temple was constructed with a central 'mammisi' (birthhouse) with a walkway. There were two pylons to the north and south forming the borders of an inner courtyard. Behind the smaller pylon lay the Temple of Isis itself. In front of the larger pylon a long forecourt lead to the southern tip of the island looking out upon the water.

On the island there was actually a complex of temples which made up the whole area. Cleopatra prayed at the outside Kiosk of Nectanbo, devoted to Hathor, goddess of music and harmony, its shrines and sistrum pillars depicting four sided cows' heads with ears, which represented her dominion over north, south, east and west.

They moved slowly through the outer pylons and inner courtyard. A long, shaded colonnade provided respite from the heat, while wall openings gave tantalising glimpses through to blue water sparkling in the sunlight. The beauty of the setting was undeniable.

Cleopatra went alone up the steps from the courtyard into the temple. Her gaze was drawn to an ornately engraved door mantle relief of the great god, Horus. She passed further into the temple past the huge carved columns.

As she studied the reliefs of the great goddess Isis holding the ankh - the key of life, she marvelled at her beauty and her power. The temple carvings were some of the most graceful and feminine in Egypt. Here, the female was represented often, showing not only grace but power.

Cleopatra's own responsibility for the welfare of Caesarion and her people, now sat with an even greater burden on her shoulders. She could expect help from no one except the gods.

Side by side in the temples of her people, the papyrus and the lotus appeared together, - the male with the female, - one without the other being incomplete, - the two equally together, a perfect whole. Now she had lost Caesar and she stood alone.

'Isis give me the strength I need, for I am not strong enough alone!' she prayed. As if in answer to her entreaty, as she left the temple, she saw on the western pylon tower an inscription which read '*...I will strengthen your arm against your enemies...' (Horus)*

Cleopatra returned to Alexandria content that she was ready for the next episode of her life, whatever that might be.

Chapter 8

EPHESUS
43BC

Julius Caesar's prized legion. The Ninth. It was forever his own identity, thought Suetonius. He had retired now, in 46 BC - after the campaigns in Spain and Africa. For his trouble he carried a nasty scar down one side of his face, and a body that was older than his years. But at least he had known what pride was. And despite what had happened, he still did!

Caesar's 'Baby', the favourite Ninth. Suetonius' mind returned to the horrors of the civil war against Pompey. Soldiers who should have known better - soldiers who knew well that no Roman soldier ever turned his back on a battle or disobeyed orders - had committed mutiny. And it had been Caesar's Ninth Legion.

They were taught a lesson no legion would ever forget.

Were the Ninth really decimated? He had heard the very idea of it questioned by others who came after them. Surely that could not be? But the Roman army's superiority came from the very thing that they had abandoned. Discipline. No other Roman soldier after them would ever be allowed to make that mistake again. Roman commanders were tough. They had to be.

Lots were drawn. Every tenth man was killed by his 'brothers' with their bare hands. Those who were not drawn out by lot and survived, remembered always, and so did every other legion. Eventually the Ninth legion regrouped in 48 BC.

Suetonius, still strong and fit, lived in a village in the foothills of Rome. It was a quiet but peaceful life after his years of fighting. He was alone, and could have wished that was not the case, but as yet, had found no one with whom to share his life. At least when he woke each day he saw the wooded hillsides, a lovely, small temple to Vesta on the crest of one, and heard the splashing of a waterfall down the side of another.

Extra money would have helped. He barely made enough to feed himself and keep one of the very old, small houses that stood in a narrow alleyway off the main thoroughfare. He had become well known to the locals and neighbours and found the place quaint, with a sleepy cat or two wandering down the alleys and the occasional drunk making his way home. Suetonius had found a place he enjoyed calling his home.

Then he was contacted by an old friend who worked in the city for a somewhat questionable acquaintance, and they needed a job done. An assassination.

This was not the sort of work Suetonius wanted. But the money was so extravagant, he could not afford to refuse the opportunity. His expenses were paid and a good wage. He travelled to Ephesus and took up lodgings in a small lodging house at the upper end of Arcadian Street, near the Theatre. His instructions were simply, to wait.

And wait he did, for many months. It didn't unduly worry him as he was being paid to just look around the town and enjoy himself, which he also did, often at one of the inns. Finally the summons came. He was given the name of the victim and the location. It would not be overly exaggerating to say that he was surprised. But a job was a job, and it had to be done.

—

Morning on this day in Ephesus dawned with wispy, white candy floss clouds delicately spread across the sky. As the day wore on they thickened and scudded from sight pushed by a stiff breeze. By evening as the breeze died, heavy storm clouds hung over the city.

The procession of Artemis – Goddess of Ephesus, was the focal point of the year, and the beginning of a month of joyful celebrations and festivities for the people. The tradition was as old as memory itself, and a cause of pride for the Ephesians. Visitors from far and wide attended what was for many of them a once in a lifetime pilgrimage, and the city grew even richer from the additional demand for food and lodging.

For most citizens today was a holiday. Everyone relaxed and it was usual to prepare a large, celebratory meal, usually at dinner, for family and friends to enjoy in their homes. Kitchens were busy with preparations, cooking the special treats reserved for the occasion.

The Temple of Artemis stood over a mile from the city and as the people in Ephesus watched that evening, a long line of flares blazed a path through the darkness slowly heading towards them. The processional route was semi circular, passing all of the main vantage points, and crowds lined the streets eager for a glimpse of the much venerated statue and images, and of the long line of robed priests.

It took over an hour for the whole procession to pass. Arsinoe and the other guests of the Temple watched the start of the procession, but even on this occasion were unable to venture outside. One by one they returned to their rooms until Arsinoe found herself alone in the large, open visitors' area which gave entry to the inner temple shrine.

On passing through the city walls the priests wound their way past residential insulae, the U shaped heroon depicting Androclus killing a wild boar – the foundation story of Ephesus, - and the Memmius monument dedicated to the dictator Sulla's grandson. On past the Bouleuterion theatre of the Senate with its wooden roof they walked, past the State Agora and the Prytanean. Then they continued on Curetes Street and down to Marble Street and the Theatre.

People danced and sang and there was a general feeling of festivity. Children had been brought to watch by their parents as a special outing. One small boy cowering behind his mother was crying.

'The statue is so ugly Mama, I'm scared!'

'You must not say things like that,' - the mother quickly soothed her son. - 'The goddess will hear you!'

Everywhere there was a feeling of hope for the future.

—

The quietness was total. Flares penetrated the darkness, throwing light and shadow,—still leaving most of the inside of the Temple surrounding them in blackness. Arsinoe peered ahead of her towards the central shrine. She could just make out the wooden statue of Artemis which leered out at her like some monstrous gargoyle. 'I would give anything to be back in Egypt,' she whispered to herself. 'How has my life brought me to this, an exile in a land where I do not belong? I have lost everything except my very existence, and even that is not certain.'

The attack when it came, was swift and silent!

A strong arm went around Arsinoe's throat from behind and she felt a sharp knife pressed against her skin. 'Cleopatra sends you her love,' whispered the assassin. The moment was broken as one of the Korai stepped into view from behind a column close by.

'You will not defile the Temple with an act of violence!' She commanded, her voice ringing with authority throughout the Temple.

Startled, as the girl stepped closer to them, the assassin pushed Arsinoe aside, stabbing the Korai as he fled. She fell, blood staining her white robe crimson. Arsinoe, her face ashen screamed for help which brought others running to their aid. The young girl bled to death on the Temple's white marble floor. Distraught, Arsinoe collapsed to her knees next to the girl who had shown courage beyond her years and the ultimate conviction in her beliefs.

When the priests returned bearing the statue of Artemis, they found a scene of indescribable horror. It was said that a faint outline of the handmaiden's blood forever remained on the Temple floor. The goddess had not been able to protect one of her own.

The next morning a leaden sky still hung over the city, the rain poured down and the wind whipped up the seas off the coastline. The High Priest called together all who had witnessed the murder scene. Distraught, he faced them in the silence.

'I require all here to take a vow before the goddess that not a word of the tragedy last night will pass your lips. Is there anyone who will not take the oath?' Silence. He continued. 'We have been blessed by the goddess in that, fortunately, no outsiders were present. We cannot, however, allow the sanctity of the Temple to be compromised in any way, especially when so many pilgrims travel so far to pay homage to the goddess. We can only pray that news of this tragedy does not become known.'

Amunet arrived to find Arsinoe not terrified and depressed, but in a state of steely calm and determination. 'I've been sitting throughout the night,' she said, 'thinking about what I must do to save my life. Together, and with some help, we will put the plan that I have decided on into action.

Antony was so close to Caesar, that there is a risk he may become close also to my sister. Lepidus does not have the support or military backing to compete with the other two. Therefore, I must try to trade with Octavian.

It breaks my heart to even think about giving a Roman such a precious, ancient icon passed down to the most pure blooded descendant of the Ptolemy dynasty throughout our history for hundreds of years, but I fear I have no option.'

She took Amunet to sit on the side of her bed with her. 'It would be almost impossible to reach Octavian with a message directly, without disclosing my identity and why I wish to speak with him. Someone close to him would be better.

There are rumours that Marcus Agrippa returns soon to Rome, to supervise a building and restoration program Octavian is planning to start for the city. Apparently it will be extensive, as he feels that Rome's buildings are not in a condition that reflects its present position of power and prestige. They will need senior supervisory sculptors with reputations for experience working on other great buildings.

I have noticed two Roman sculptors and restorers who work here in the temple and occasionally stopped to admire their work. Amunet, find out the name and everything you can about the older, dark haired man, including the name of his patron. I believe he may be an ideal messenger to speak with Agrippa about work on the new buildings in Rome, while at the same time approaching him with an offer from me to present to Octavian. While you are gone, I will decide how to best make the necessary arrangements.

Oh, and Amunet, also find out who runs the foremost protection service in the city, could carry out surveillance and, shall we say, silence someone if the need arose, then keep his mouth shut!'

CHAPTER 9

42BC

THE CELSUS LIBRARY, two stories high, slender and delicately feminine in style, was thought to be one of the most beautiful buildings in Ephesus. It stood at the junction of Curetes and Marble Streets. Statues gracing its exterior represented wisdom, knowledge, intelligence and valour – all highly appropriate for the purpose of such a building.

Gaius strode up the front steps and into the main reading room, which was much admired for the coloured marble covering its walls and floor. He was eager to use the library's scrolls.

'Good Morning, Publius.' Gaius smiled at the young library attendant who was well known to him.

'I don't see you in here so often these days,' Publius replied, 'but I suppose I wouldn't be either if I had a wife like Julia to spend my time with!'

'Well, she's given me time off for a couple of hours today,' laughed Gaius, 'so I had better make the most of it. I'm looking for scrolls on Greek sculpture to help with a design for Lucius' villa. A little inspiration would certainly help! Will you see what you can find for me?'

Publius hurried away as Gaius took one of the reading areas.

The library had in excess of 12,000 scrolls, exceeded in number only by the cities of Pergamon and Alexandria, so Gaius was hopeful of finding something suitable to inspire him. He treasured this rare time for research and was soon happily reading through the selections found by Publius.

An intelligent and well read man, Gaius Domitius had been born in the suburbs of Rome to an artisan father and a young woman who had disappointed her wealthy merchant class family, by marrying a man thought to be beneath her station in life.

From his father, Gaius inherited his artistic talent. From his mother, came a lifelong love of the classics, history and the theatre. By nature he could be impatient and demanding, especially with his work, but he was rarely impulsive. He was disciplined, loyal and honest.

The time passed quickly. He felt a tap on the shoulder and found Sextus looking down at him.

'Don't forget, we promised Livia and Julia to take them shopping and get something to eat, – they're waiting downstairs for us.'

Gaius returned his scrolls and the two men wandered down to meet their wives, then made their way through the arched Gates of Mazeus and Mithridates into the commercial Agora.

What they did not see was the man lounging by the side of the archway watching them intently, who followed them as they shopped.

Lucius Verres was a very wealthy man who spent his money wisely. He was also of the opinion that he couldn't take it with him when finally called to account by the gods. Consequently, he had long ago made a conscious decision to enjoy those things in life which brought him comfort, beauty and anything else he really desired. A large man with a pleasant enough face, he dressed in fine clothes and owned a magnificent villa. There was only one thing he hungered for that had so far escaped him, - and that was power!

A surprise visitor had arrived at his villa some hours before, a beautiful Egyptian girl. Bowing low she handed him a sealed scroll.

'Good Morning, Sir. My name is Amunet. I have been sent by the Princess Arsinoe to hand you this message. She requests that you be so kind as to read it and keep the information it contains confidential. I will return for your written reply at this time tomorrow.'

Lucius had heard rumours of Arsinoe's residing at the Temple but wondered why she would choose to correspond with him. So it was with some interest that he opened the seal. Intrigued he began to read, his shock mounting with every passing line. The message read:

To Lucius Verres

Greetings!

You no doubt know who I am. I have a proposal for you given in the strictest confidence. My enquiries inform me that you are a man of discretion and I am in need of such a man to trust with an important task.

I am also aware that you are the patron of the sculptor called Gaius. I require a trustworthy messenger to send to Rome to contact a person of high standing. I doubt that Gaius would accept such a commission if offered directly, as his wife is here in Ephesus and he is also answerable to you for his time in working under your patronage.

My request is that you, as his patron, order him to visit Rome to deliver a message. He is in no position to refuse your order. I will inform you of to whom it is to be given should you accept this proposal- and Gaius may then simply return to Ephesus.

He will visit Rome on the pretext of seeking work on the city's new building program. He will not know the contents of the message.

I expect in the near future to be in a position to reward your assistance to me most generously. As you are aware, Marcus Antonius presently holds the position of Governor of Ephesus. That does not always have to be so! I'm sure you understand my meaning! Please send your reply, I will prove most appreciative of your help in this matter.

Arsinoe -Princess of the Kingdom of Egypt

Lucius handed his reply to the messenger the next day as requested. It read simply:

To My Lady Arsinoe

Greetings!

If you will provide me with the message, details of to whom it is to be given in Rome and when you wish your request to be carried out, I will be delighted to assist you with the utmost discretion.

With Respect
Lucius Verres

—

Gaius had two passions in his life. One of them was sculpting. He thought himself extremely lucky that his work was something from which he gained not only a living, but also the fulfilment that came from creative expression. Since arriving in Ephesus he had enjoyed freedom most of the time, in the way he chose to sculpt the commissions he received through his patron, Lucius Verres.

Without a doubt, he most enjoyed sculpting marble statues, and his name as a sculptor was quickly becoming well known. He innately understood always, that all forms of art are a means of communication, whether through music or sculpture. But that was simply the beginning.

Gaius had seen countless statues that lacked the very quality that defined what was special from what was not, - and that was the emotion or 'spirit' of the piece. Many were cold and lifeless, and not just through poor technical execution. It was 'feeling,' - exultation, pain, joy, arrogance or anger – emotion, was what gave the work life!

He liked the malleable feel of the marble under his hands as he began to shape it, allowing him to create the softly flowing folds in the dress of a goddess, or the sensitivity in the fingers of a hand. For every sculptor, though, there were times now and again, when a mistake threatened to undo all the prior effort that had gone into what had already been completed.

He was correcting such a fault with the placement of a foot, when breathless and panting from the steep run up Curetes Street to the State Agora, one of the shabby young street urchins who eked out a living by running messages for the rich, shoved a scroll into his hand, then took off again at full pace back down the way he had come. Gaius opened the scroll.

The message was brief and precise:

> *'Gaius, please attend the Baths this afternoon promptly one hour before dusk!'*
>
> *Lucius Verres*

'I wonder what he wants?' Sextus glanced across at Gaius with a frown as they packed up their tools for the day.

'I hope we haven't slipped up on some work somewhere.' Gaius also looked uneasy.

'Well, I guess I'll know soon enough. Let's hope we still have our jobs tomorrow!'

Both knew that it was highly unusual for Lucius to socialise with either of them. Their relationship was purely patron and employee. Arriving at the Baths, Gaius found Lucius already preparing to enter the warm water of the tepidarium.

The Baths of Scholastica, located at the lower end of Curetes Street, were situated on the second and third storeys of the building. It featured high, arched doorways and comfortable fittings. Its central location ensured its popularity right across all classes, and patrons were numerous. The massage area upstairs always had clients waiting to have their aches and pains pummelled away, - hopefully - and its proximity to the brothel services was no accident. Gaius had hurried to get there on time. Now he approached Lucius Verres swiftly and with some misgivings.

'Gaius, I have an important task for you to perform which will mean your absence from the city for a time,' he announced.

'You will be taking a short journey. Come to the villa tomorrow morning before you commence work, and I will give you the necessary details. I thought it best to let you know now so you can prepare your wife for your absence.'

With that, Lucius raised his hand in dismissal and their discussion was at an end.

The Baths were busy, as usual, as this was always one of the social hubs of Ephesus. Colourfully decorated walls, and comfortable surroundings, provided a place for both business and pleasure for all classes.

Many workers began work early and took most of the afternoon off, thereby avoiding working in the worst of the afternoon's heat in summer, but allowing them to relax in the luxurious warmth of the tepidarium or the hot area, the caldarium, inside the Baths.

Relieved to have escaped any of his feared outcomes from the meeting, Gaius got out of the building as quickly as possible. He headed home by way of Sextus' house so he could set his friend's mind at peace and also ask him to watch over Julia.

Everything had happened in a blur, thought Gaius the next day. Having called at Lucius Verres' villa he had been given an excellent work reference, money and the name of a house of lodging in Rome. He was also given a sealed message which he was told not to open.

He was instructed to apply to the new building site in the city, a temple, and insist on handing the message personally to Marcus Agrippa, and no one else. Gaius was somewhat surprised but supposed that somehow Agrippa must be known to Lucius.

Within days he was boarding a ship headed for the Roman city of Brundisium. After an uneventful journey the ship entered the natural deer's head shaped harbour and he disembarked. It was a large city with a bustling commercial port.

It was early morning, and not yet overly busy. A few people sat around next to their belongings to discourage theft, waiting to embark on a ship, and the usual, scraggy beggars had taken up their accustomed places, ready for a day of disappointment. Waiting in front of vessels sat consignments of goods in huge amphorae. The crews had begun to load them. Unable to stand, each on their own, these containers were, however, ideal for transporting merchandise. Placed in an area of the ship to provide balance, their shape enabled them to be stacked tightly together in rows, and also one row on top of another.

Gaius was ravenously hungry. He decided to walk to the fringes of the dock, looking for a caupona. As he walked, a 'fishy' smell wafted towards him. Ahead, he saw large vats, and on approaching them, realised they contained whole, small fish heavily laced with salt. They had started to decompose, a process that would be accelerated once the heat of the sun strengthened. Already, the contents had begun to liquefy into the addictive, expensive, most sort after Roman delicacy, known as 'Garum.' That lot would be worth a few aurei, he thought. Catching sight of a caupona, he entered, and sat down to eat, after which, he decided to set out for Rome.

'Where is the start of the Via Appia to Rome?' he enquired of a nearby local.

'Up the hill there and look for the two tall pillars,' he was told.

It was not long before Gaius had found the pillars and paid a cart owner taking goods to Rome, for a place in the back jolting along with the amphorae.

Named after its builder, the Via Appia was the foremost example of Rome's road building skills and the template for foreign roads that became a major part of her arsenal in conquering her enemies. Gaius appreciated the engineering genius of the great aqueducts that lined the route like giant sentinels. They provided life giving waters to quench Rome's thirst, and water for hygiene and social needs, such as public baths and fountains. Some of the rich with their high status villas outside Rome owned carp pools, which they delighted in showing off to elite visitors. More importantly, without the water running through the great aqueducts, some of Rome's most essential industries, would cease to exist.

He marvelled at the construction of the road itself. Straight, and passing through agricultural countryside, it was busy and carried every sort of traveller of the time, including the great marching armies of Rome. Even though he would miss Julia, Gaius looked forward with some excitement to checking out the new building works in the city.

As they neared Rome, Gaius passed by the many tombs of the elite which lined the roadway, including the fortress like mausoleum dedicated to Cecilia Metellus. As with other cities, the dead of the Capital were also buried outside the city walls. The area lining the Via Appia was frequented by the homeless, thieves and other more sinister characters. Too many corpses were dumped here to count, and these were murder victims, who now joined those peacefully laid to rest after funerals. Travellers hurried by, mindless of those who had preceded them in life. This was especially not the place to loiter after dark. At night, the section of the Via Appia leading to the Capena Gate was one of quiet, deadly menace.

Riding a little distance behind the cart, Sargon, a good horseman, was also enjoying this change of scene from his usual day to day activities. He had received an offer from Princess Arsinoe too good to reject, to ensure Gaius' physical safety, watch where he went and what he did while in Rome, then follow him back to Ephesus. Having hired some extra 'muscle' in Brundisium in the form of an ex gladiator, Sargon, who was quite an expert himself with a knife, did not expect to have too much trouble.

Chapter 10

ROME
42BC

Agrippa was in a foul mood! His tooth ached and he'd had enough of dealing with labourers and artisans. A raucous clamouring reached his ears coming from the main entry gate to the site. It seemed someone was having a heated argument at full volume.

'Cacat! Tell them to get the hell out of there!' He yelled at his assistant Quintus who turned tail and ran at full pelt to the gate.

'Tace! What in the name of all the gods is going on?' Quintus roared.

The site supervisor sneered at Gaius. 'This imbecile is insisting on delivering a message to Marcus Agrippa in person,' he announced. Gaius handed his work reference to Quintus who read it and being suitably impressed, decided to risk taking Gaius to Agrippa's tent.

Gaius saw a well built, young but weary looking soldier not particularly pleased at the interruption.

'Well, what is your business here?' he demanded gruffly, looking Gaius up and down,

'Sir, I am to hand you this message and request that it be given safely into the hands of Caesar Octavian.'

He handed the message to Agrippa who demanded,

'Who is this message from?'

'Lucius Verres, Sir.' replied Gaius.

'I don't know any Lucius Verres, is this some kind of joke?'

Gaius met steely blue eyes boring into his and felt the full impact of the other man's commanding personality.

'Quintus, have him taken to the Carcer until we find out what this is all about,' ordered Agrippa.

Gaius was shocked to find himself promptly marched away under guard through the building site gate, much to the amusement and heckling of the site supervisor, and through the Forum to the 'Carcer' prison. A two storey structure, it stood at the far end of the Forum around a corner by the Senate House, beneath the hill of the Capitol.

Gaius stumbled as he was roughly pushed through the door into the upper storey. Dimly lit and with a low ceiling the space was suffocatingly confining. Constructed out of roughly hewn rock, it held the smell of death and was a place of despair.

It was the last place on earth that was seen by those such as Vercingetorix, who had the audacity to lead rebellions against Rome, only to be conquered. After the ordeal of being dragged behind their conqueror in a Triumph, they ended up slaughtered in the prison.

'Come to us for a stay have you?' Rufus, the legionary on duty snarled. He glanced across at the escorting soldiers.

'What are the orders?'

'He's only to be confined for the night until further notice,' was the reply.

'That's a pity.' Rufus grimaced.

With that the escort left and Gaius was unceremoniously shoved into a corner next to the wall.

'You're lucky, you know,' remarked Rufus. 'See that hole there? That goes down below us into the Tullianum. That's for those who are to be strangled and then their bodies thrown into the sewer, - so don't accidentally fall in, will you!'

Rufus laughed uproariously at his own little joke and Gaius thought he was going to vomit. Over the long day and night to come, he said nothing and barely moved until the escort came back for him the next morning.

Watching nearby, Sargon had been alarmed to see Gaius disappearing under guard. He could do little except follow at a distance to see where Gaius was being taken. Aware that nothing could be done until the next morning, he decided to take a tour of the city to see what might be of interest. Sargon had never visited Rome before, and his steps quickened with excitement as he walked the short distance back towards the central area of the Forum Romanum.

Already bustling with vendors, senators, soldiers, law advocates and numerous others, the Forum opened before him like a magic box. Riveted to the spot, his eyes were dazzled by the magnificence of the scene.

The Vestal Temple; House of the Pontifex Maximus; Temples of Jupiter, Bellona, Apollo and Saturn and public buildings such as the Basilica

Aemilia all spread out before him. Now, for the first time, he understood why it was called the greatest city in the world.

The Vestal Temple was particularly lovely. It was small, but one of the most graceful of all Rome's temples. It was the place of worship for six Vestal Virgins who guarded Rome's perpetual flame. The flame must never be allowed to become extinguished, or the city's safety would be compromised. They spent their young lives in the service of the goddess Vesta, and when they grew older, having spent thirty years at the Temple, were discharged from their duties with a pension and the grateful thanks of the city.

Adjacent to the Temple stood the vestals' accommodation. This area was reserved for females only, except for the Pontifex Maximus, the official High Priest. The convent in which the vestals lived was large, gracious and gleaming. There were colonnades lined with classical, marble statues, rooms for each girl and servants, and an area where they conducted their duties receiving and safeguarding wills. Outsiders walking by glimpsed the blue of a reflecting pool, and, in addition, a formally laid out garden. The colours and fragrance provided a feast for the senses when the garden's roses were in bloom.

The noise jarred his senses and the cries of the vendors - '*Special prices this morning, the best honey in the city,*' shook him out of his reverie, as he found himself jostled by the ever increasing numbers making their way through the Via Sacra. The Palatine Hill looked like a quiet, green oasis in the chaos, but he decided to turn his steps in the other direction instead.

Exiting the Forum on the Via Argiletum near the Basilica Aemilia he found himself among booksellers and upmarket antique dealers, wool merchants, and a Jewish Synagogue. These businesses all looked busy and prosperous.

The insulae he found in the Subura area, unlike those in Ephesus, were obviously mainly for the very poor. Two or three stories high and built of wood, each dwelling consisted of only one or two rooms crammed full of people.

There was a constant fire hazard due to accidents from burning candles, and only the ground floor of each building had running water, heating or a toilet. Sargon made his way carefully, having seen the contents of a slop pail thrown with vigour from a top floor apartment land in the street, just in front of his feet.

Returning to the Forum and climbing the Capitoline Hill, he descended on the other side and walking on, came across narrow alleyways, many of them unnamed, alive with the early morning activity of slaves going about their masters' business.

Many were headed for the bakeries or markets, or delivering messages. Litters went by their curtains tightly closed. Occasionally groups of drunken gladiators passed him coming out of the inns, of which there were many, or street thugs looking for trouble.

His curiosity turned to amazement at the sight of Pompey's Theatre. One of the more recent structures in Rome, built some ten years before, Sargon saw that it was absolutely huge and built of stone, thus making it permanent rather than the usual temporary wooden structures. It was here, he knew, in the attached assembly hall that Julius Caesar had been murdered. He decided to return to his lodging house to rest before venturing out again later.

Night fell like a cloak of black velvet thrown carelessly over the city, - hiding its grimy secrets. The most popular pastime in the Subura was theft. Even the street lamps were not immune, leaving the alleyways bereft of light and less than enticing. Murder, shady deals and prostitution flourished in the streets and inside seedy brothels. Taking care not to step in anything of a questionable nature, Sargon wandered again down the winding, filthy and narrow laneways, many stinking of excrement. Ordering his gladiator protector to 'shadow' him as a protection against robbery or murder, he roamed the un-named alleyways, estimating the number of brothels and the type of customers each attracted.

Deciding to check out one or two of the brothels to compare them with his own establishments, he spent an enjoyable night until returning to the Carcer the next morning to see whether Gaius would be released.

Sargon was particularly happy as he was in no doubt whatsoever, that the brothels he ran in Ephesus were not only equal to, but excelled those in Rome itself!

—

Octavian's villa on the Palatine Hill was located in the prime location for a Roman patrician and many senators enjoyed the view from their villas on the high, lush green hill overlooking the Forum and the Circus Maximus. Octavian, by choice, had a modestly sized residence, preferring simplicity rather than the usual ostentation.

Octavian and Agrippa enjoyed a leisurely, relaxing dinner, drinking watered wine accompanied by an excellent array of foods, fruits and desserts. They were the closest of friends. There was no one Octavian trusted more in terms of both his personal and professional life.

Discussing how each had spent the day, Agrippa recounted the incident at the site tent and drew the message from his toga. He twirled it in the air nonchalantly.

'Probably some fool petitioning for a favour,' he laughed, and threw the scroll to Octavian. Casually, Octavian opened the message his face growing grave as he read the contents.

'Marcus, who gave you this?' He enquired.

'Some sculptor pretending to be seeking work.' Agrippa replied. 'I let him cool his heels in the Carcer for the night.'

Octavian dismissed the servants and closed the doors to the room.

'Marcus, this message is from Princess Arsinoe in Ephesus. She proposes an alliance with me against her sister Cleopatra to restore Arsinoe to the Egyptian throne as an official F*riend and Ally of Rome* and she requests that I return the messenger to Ephesus with my reply. She offers me in return one of the most powerful symbols of authority this world has ever known. Ownership would ensure that no other man could compete with me for the title of the greatest leader in the Roman world.'

Octavian fell silent, gazing into the distance. He did not disclose to Agrippa what it was that Arsinoe had offered. There were some things best kept even from one's closest friend.

Sargon was relieved to see Gaius taken from the prison the next morning and returned to Agrippa's tent. Gaius left soon after carrying a scroll, and having removed his belongings from his lodgings, returned to Brundisium from where he took passage on a ship bound for Ephesus. Sargon returned on the same ship.

—

TURKEY
Ephesus

Immediately on returning, Gaius took the message to Lucius at his villa then hurried home to a relieved Julia with a tale to tell of his meeting with Agrippa and a night in the prison. Little did he realise that the real story behind his journey was so much more than he knew.

He found Julia very agitated, which was unlike her. She was worried about their friends Livia and Sextus. For some time Livia's older sister, Servilia, had been very unwell, and had been sent to the healing centre of Aesklepion in the hope that some cure could be found. A message had arrived in Gaius' absence to say that her condition had worsened, and there was concern that she might not recover.

She had some time before, discovered a large swelling in her abdomen, and doctors feared an abnormal growth. Unmarried and childless, now that her parents had died, she had only Livia and Sextus to comfort her.

'Gaius, I know you have only just returned home, but could we possibly follow them to the centre in case we can be of some help?' Julia asked. Gaius sighed, he was tired and had been through a great deal of stress during his time away, but he was reluctant to refuse help to their close friends.

'We can leave tomorrow morning, but tonight I must get some sleep.' Julia nodded her understanding.

Neither of them had been to Aesklepion before, and had hoped they would never have to go there at all. It was, however, well known for its Snake Cult, the snake being the symbol of wisdom.

When Julia and Gaius arrived, they found to their surprise that the Centre stood in quiet, natural countryside connected to the city of Pergamon by a column lined pathway.

The Centre had a philosophy of healing which they had never heard of before. They had expected to find treatment rooms and accommodation, which in fact, they did. It was the other areas which came as a surprise.

The sick were aided in their recovery by attention to easing both mind and body together, as much as possible. Consequently, there was a theatre where performances were held to take their minds off their problems, and there were other recreational pursuits as well. A spacious and pleasant Agora with shaded resting places stood at the centre of the complex as well as a very pretty fountain. A sacred well, library and temple of Aesclepius, completed the facilities.

Livia ran to meet them as soon as she saw them from the window of her sister's room.

'Thank you so much for coming! Things have been very upsetting. Its doubtful Servilia will recover, but she is being cared for with a great deal of love and attention. The carers are wonderful!'

Julia hugged her, as Gaius made his way to find Sextus.

'Gaius, there is one special place I would like to show you and Julia,' Sextus said. 'Come, I'll show you.'

Entering down several steps leading off the area near the theatre was a tunnel. The relaxing sound of running water could be heard flowing along the purpose built channels on the ground at both sides of the pathway.

At various intervals the tunnel ceiling revealed openings to let in the sunlight and dispel the gloom.

'I've been told by the staff that they whisper words of hope down to the sick as they go down this tunnel, to help them with the treatments they are to undergo.' Sextus explained.

As they reached the end of the tunnel he led them into numerous, spacious treatment areas. 'I hope none of us ever finds ourselves here, regardless.'

Sextus turned and led the way back out of the tunnel.

—

Gaius glanced across at Julia. Her hair shone in the sun like spun gold. Sensing him watching her, she turned and smiled at him. Her smile held the sunshine within it. A smile that was for him alone. His heart skipped a beat as he realised how very much he loved her. Noting how pale she was, Gaius determined to bring some happiness into her day.

'You know, don't you, that we're very close to Pergamon here? He said.

'Yes, I suppose we must be.' She looked across at him.

'Well, as we've never been there, perhaps it's time we went,' he replied, smiling.

With lighter hearts and quicker steps they made their way towards Pergamon which they could visit on their way home to Ephesus. Long before they reached the city, they saw the huge, ancient and almost vertical Greek theatre that dominated the landscape, and could be seen for miles.

'Livia told me about their visit to see *Antigone* at home,' she said in awe, 'but it must be really something to see a play here!'

They walked through the entry tunnel into the theatre, taking seats half way towards the centre. The rows of seats dropped vertically down in a dizzying drop to the stage below, offering magnificent views not only of the stage but also the surrounding countryside. Continuing on up the very steep slope they came to the Acropolis. Gaius was, of course, anxious to see the Library and delighted when he finally entered the building. Here was the second largest collection of scrolls In the world, second only to Alexandria. Delightedly he wandered around looking at as much as possible.

'I hope nothing ever happens to this treasure of knowledge,' he murmured to Julia. 'We will have to come back here again.'

He was like a child, thought Julia. So engrossed that for him, time had stopped. She loved the frown of concentration on his face, and the delight he showed in his findings. It had been a good idea to detour here to such an interesting place.

The Greek goddess Athena protected this city, and it was to her temple that they turned next, and, entering, offered up a prayer to the goddess for their friend's sister, Servilia.

Julia and Gaius returned to Ephesus, grateful for the pleasure of their return journey, and that they did not to have health problems themselves. They knew, however, that their close friends would almost certainly soon have to face the grief of losing Servilia.

—

Lucius Verres had wasted no time in sending the message from Gaius on to Arsinoe.

'My Lady, your hands are trembling' sympathised Amunet as they sat looking at the scroll. 'Surely it will be good news!'

Arsinoe squeezed her maid's hand, 'I'm almost afraid to read it,' she replied. 'If Octavian does not understand fully the nature of what I am offering, he could well refuse me protection, but at least I know he received the message safely, and that is a promising beginning!'

Opening the scroll she read:

To Princess Arsinoe of Egypt

Greetings,

I trust you are in good health and being well served at the temple. Your proposition is, indeed, of great interest and be assured it shall receive my full attention. You should realise, however, that the timing for such a venture is, at present, somewhat premature. With your agreement, I shall contact you again when certain events have been finalised, with a view to further discussion.

With respect
Caesar Octavianus

Arsinoe's hopes rose. The letter was positive enough to raise her spirits. 'Just don't take too long, Octavian,' she whispered. 'Don't take too long.'

Chapter 11

A malignant storm swept its black waters over the merchant ship as it reared and fell violently in the waves' huge peaks and troughs. Rain teemed down angrily from clouds spewing lightening from the gods, and the ocean's menace had no ending. Everything went spinning in a giant vortex sucking and pulling them down, – down. Then came a monstrous mountain of water terrible to behold. It shook the very timbers of the ship in sheer fury, until they disintegrated and descended down the portal of a watery hell.

—

Her earliest memory was fear.

It went with her wherever she was and never completely left her side. Fear was part of nearly every waking day and decided for her much of what she did or did not say. Not that Julia said anything much, especially at the time of her earliest remembering.

She sang to herself. She rarely spoke. Singing brought her peace and was virtually the only joy in her days.

Julia was the only child of Petronius and Cornelia. Keeping largely to herself, she strove to be inconspicuous so as not to bring unwanted attention to whatever it was she was doing. She learned early that if she ever really enjoyed an activity, it was taken away from her. A quiet child, she prayed often to the gods and learned very young to read the classics, which she sometimes did for hours every day.

'Julia, you're nothing but a nuisance to this family. Come here and make yourself useful by holding this piece of cloth up for me!'

Her mother pushed her violently onto the nearest couch.

'Yes, Mama.'

'Hold it still, - you stupid girl! Lift it further from the floor!'

A sharp, stinging slap caught her across the face.

Her mother's cold glare fell upon her and Julia shuddered. Older now, she recognised the signs which predicted the onset of calculated, violent episodes which were the worst periods of her mother's aggressiveness towards her.

Things were always worst when her father was away. A Tribune in the Roman Army, he spent long periods of time away from home. Although providing them with the means to keep a respectable house in the suburbs of Rome, Julia felt she hardly knew him.

Petronius was a quiet, withdrawn man. Very private. What he wanted was a quiet home as a respite from the violent life of the battlefront. Intelligent and well educated, he was a good looking man who had married a little older than most of his generation.

Julia knew she would pay for it later whenever some Roman matron, unthinking, remarked upon Julia's beauty, saying as a compliment.

'Well, she obviously got her beauty from her father.'

Julia's mother was a plain woman whose only claim to any beauty was the rather unusual colour of her wavy, thick hair. Cornelia had taken more and more to episodes of striking Julia with a rod until she was screaming in pain and covered in purple welts on her body over those parts of her always covered by clothing. Sick at heart, Julia felt she had nowhere to turn.

And then came the news that she had dreaded.

Petronius had been killed on the battlefield in Gaul. There were no tears from Cornelia. Theirs had been a loveless marriage. But now a new problem arose. How were they to survive? Her father's brother stepped in as the new head of the family and after a suitable period of mourning for Cornelia, arranged an appropriate marriage.

Julia's stepfather was a kindly man, many years older than her father had been. Praxus had recently been widowed and was looking to marry again to a respectable matron. He liked Julia, now herself about to reach an age to be married, and his kindness to her improved her life immensely.

A well to do wine and luxury goods merchant, Praxus' ships travelled from Brundisium to Athens, Ephesus and even up to the area of the Black Sea. He, himself, remained in Rome, thus providing a secure and safe environment and more emotional support for Julia than she had ever known.

With her beauty, Julia had received several good offers of marriage but had refused them all. Her young life had been so deprived of love that she had decided to wait for the special man who would give her what she valued most. In the meantime, she enjoyed many outings with her stepfather. He supported her wish to wait for the marriage that was right for her.

'Papa! May I come to the shipping offices with you today?'

'Yes, why not?' he would reply. 'And while we are there we will go to the fishmongers and choose some nice pieces of fish for our dinner.'

For some time life was pleasant and the gods smiled on them. Then, one morning, a messenger came to see Praxus at their home. His newest, most expensive ship, on which he still owed a large loan, had been lost in a terrible storm at sea, not far from Athens. The crew were all unaccounted for, and all the luxury goods with which the ship had been laden had all been lost.

Although this type of loss was always a possibility, every shipping merchant owner prayed to the god Jupiter that it would never happen to them. But now the worst had indeed happened.

It was soon after this incident that Julia had met and fallen in love with Gaius. They had not been long in Ephesus when news of Praxus' sudden death reached her. She grieved for him greatly.

Julia had hustled around to the home of Livia and Sextus earlier in the afternoon having received a message that they were returning home. She had carried with her the necessary ingredients to cook a tasty, hot dinner which would be waiting for them on their return. She then set about tidying the little home they had left so abruptly.

Life really was so precious and so frail, she thought. The news of Servilia and the grief of Livia and Sextus had set her thinking back to her past and she realised how much sadness she carried inside her. It really didn't take much to set any life swirling out of control.

She took one last look at the house to see she had forgotten nothing, and then left a message for her friends. She hoped that her small act of kindness would comfort them. Then she made her way home, with little time left before Gaius returned from work.

Julia busied herself arranging the table for dinner, placing flowers in the centre and straightening up the rest of the rooms. She endeavoured to feel more positive, but the past, once roused, was hard to shake. She felt tears welling up in her eyes. The minutes seemed to drag by. She wondered if, perhaps, she should tell Gaius what was bothering her. She had no doubt he would understand. The minute she saw him come through the door, she knew she wanted nothing more than to feel his arms around her, and the support she knew he would give her. What he did not tell her, was the anger he felt, on learning what this beautiful, sensitive girl had gone through.

That night, as Gaius held her, she wept for all the pain and sadness that she had known, much of which he had been unaware of. She thanked the gods to have found him. Then she vowed to look resolutely towards happiness and the future.

Part III

'Dance as though no one is watching
Love as though you've never been hurt
Sing as though no one can hear you
Live as though heaven is on earth.'

Souza

Chapter 12

Tarsus (Cilicia)
41BC

Mark Antony, Autocrator of the Eastern Empire of the Roman world awaited Cleopatra's arrival with pleasure. He stopped fidgeting with his tunic and glanced over at one of his generals who was removing maps from the central table.

'Delius, leave them there for when Cleopatra arrives.'

Looking somewhat dubious, Delius replaced the map he had just removed.

'Marcus, you surely don't intend to discuss campaign strategies with her do you?'

Antony laughed. 'No, I wouldn't think so, but it will not disadvantage us to look as if we have been working. Make sure, will you, that the men are in position for her arrival, it also won't go astray for us to make a good general impression!'

Antony had long envied Caesar his liaison with Cleopatra. Since he had first seen her in Rome his physical longing for her had been intense. But she had belonged to Caesar. On one day, with Caesar's murder, that had all changed, but she had gone. Every other woman he met, competed with her for his heart, but he could not shake her from his memory.

He longed with every fibre of his being to run his hands over her body, to touch her hair, hear the sound of her laughter and smell her perfume. But she had seemed unattainable.

Surely, he had thought, there were too many obstacles to be overcome? Then, finally, last night, the dream had become a reality. He realised now, that there was always a way if you wanted something badly enough. It was worth any effort to reach out for what his heart told him was special, and would probably be offered to him only once in his lifetime.

Cleopatra's arrival in Tarsus had been an incredible piece of showmanship. Seated on an ornate throne aboard her lavishly decorated ship her arrival had caused mayhem. The population gaped at the gold of the Royal Barge with its ornate decoration and golden oars.

The banquet which had followed had been decadent to say the least, with Antony living up to his reputation as a follower of Dionysus, god of wine and excess. He was determined though, not to miss his opportunity with her, and sought her out afterwards.

Antony's first night with Cleopatra was everything each could ever have anticipated. Both were physically in their prime and enjoyed the intimacy and exploration of a new love. Cleopatra was an experienced seductress rather than a truly beautiful woman, small in stature but with a charisma few men could resist.

Antony was a man women loved to look at as well as to love. Broad shouldered, of average height, he was well proportioned, fit and well muscled. He was sexually a man of great appetites and exuded a very male presence. He was if anything, the complete physical opposite of the lean, tall and more intellectual Caesar. As Cleopatra found out, he was also a patient and skilful lover.

Tarsus, capital of Cilicia and a busy commercial port was perfectly positioned for the meeting of Egypt's Queen and the Roman Autocrator of the East. Close to centres such as Ephesus and Athens, yet it was far enough away to ensure reasonable privacy.

Antony rather liked the city. With an entry through a lovely arched Roman gateway, the *Sea Gate*, and roads built by Roman engineers, it provided all of his requirements even though lacking some of the sophistication of larger centres.

He had been reluctant initially to invite Cleopatra to meet with him before she had first been the one to issue an invitation. Antony was well aware, however, how desperately he needed her wealth and especially her fleet of ships. And beneath it all, lay the need to see her again.

A final encounter against Octavian could not be far away. Antony hoped to engage him in a land battle, for which Antony was certainly the most experienced and had the most talent. A sea engagement, probably pitted against Agrippa, was nowhere nearly as much to his liking. He looked up as Cleopatra swept into the command tent.

'So, my petal, did you sleep well?' He asked, smiling, as he rose to his feet.

'You should know!' Cleopatra smiled back.

'I'm surprised you're on your feet at all though, after the amount of wine you drank last night. But this afternoon we have a great deal to talk about. I'm not so deluded as to think our "discussions" last night are the only reason you're pleased to see me?'

Antony's smile faded. 'Last night is certainly a reason for me to be pleased to see you, surely, but as you seem intent on discussing more serious matters, perhaps we should begin? He stepped over to the map table and spread them out before her.

'These are our latest strategies.' Antony murmured.

Cleopatra cast her eyes over the first of the maps. She was no stranger to map reading, being experienced in strategic planning with her own generals.

'Would you like to study them more closely and let me have your opinion?'

Antony quickly discovered that this was quite a different woman from the one who had slept with him the night before. This woman knew how to negotiate as well as seduce until she got what she wanted.

Cleopatra knew that if she was to provide Antony with her patronage, it would cost her dearly in ships and gold. She was determined to get value for what she supplied. Her price politically, was the return of Cyprus and Cilicia to Egyptian rule. Her price personally, was Antony, - and Arsinoe's head.

Chapter 13

Sardis

THERE HAD BEEN very few times in the life of Lucius Verres when he had found himself lost for words. He was strongly drawn to the beautiful Egyptian woman who had become the intermediary between himself and the Princess Arsinoe. He thought Amunet not only beautiful, but a woman of quiet dignity and grace.

'Would you consider accompanying me on an outing? With the permission of your mistress, of course?' Lucius asked her with some hesitation.

'How thoughtful, I would be delighted,' she smiled. And so it was that they ventured to the elegant city of Sardis.

Lucius had chosen Sardis partly because he knew that Amunet had never been there. Also, he knew, it was a place that could be appreciated for its decorative buildings and charm. The city had flourished after falling to Roman rule, although it failed to ever again reach the prosperity it had enjoyed in the earlier time of Croesus. Somehow, it seemed the right place to take a cultured woman like Amunet. Perhaps, thought Lucius, he might even recount to her the stories of the gleaming golden coins, the citadel, and the conspirators, Brutus and Cassius, all of them part of the history of Sardis.

The countryside they passed through was peaceful enough, on the wide, fertile plain of the Gediz River Valley, although they had to contend with other travellers, as the Royal Road was a major thoroughfare. As they neared the city, they stopped to watch a group of men chopping down trees on the fringes of settlement. On Amunet's enquiring what they were building, Lucius replied that they were cutting firewood for the Roman Baths in Sardis.

After a long journey they reached the city and found a quaint, small restaurant overlooking the Royal Road. The food was surprisingly good, and, satisfied, they wandered through some of the remaining shops, with Lucius entering into a long discussion with the proprietor of Jacob's Paint Store. He finally decided on buying a vivid blue paint for the renovation of his front door.

'Where did you get this?' Lucius asked Jacob.

'It comes all the way from Susa in Persia, Sir,' the shopkeeper replied, happy to have yet another satisfied customer.

'You might try the hardware store next door. They have some really unusual front door fittings.'

Which is exactly what Lucius did, finding to his delight, exactly the right one.

After visiting the elaborately decorated bath house and admiring the huge gymnasium, they explored the Temple of Artemis complex nearby, with its Ionian columns and marble tower. Set in beautiful countryside the huge Temple held their rapt attention with the perfection of its decoration and it was some time before they were ready to leave. The day finished with a visit to the theatre and stadium.

Amunet shyly slipped her arm through her companion's. 'Thank you for inviting me, Lucius, this has been such a wonderful day.' Lucius smiled contentedly. He had never enjoyed another person's company as much as he did Amunet's, and when they parted after returning to Ephesus, it was with the promise that they would meet again very soon for what he hoped would be another of many more outings to come.

—

'Good evening, Justinia.'

'Good evening, Amunet. Did you have a pleasant day?' asked the landlady.

'Yes, thank you. It was wonderful.'

Amunet smiled at her and entered the small room in the lodging house provided for her by Arsinoe. Standing not far from the Upper Agora it was central enough for convenience, although being quite a long, brisk walk away from her mistress. Since arriving in Ephesus Amunet had been constantly in the service of Arsinoe with little time for her own leisure.

She really liked Lucius. He was kind and respectful, and treated her in a way she had thought would never be possible for her with a man, especially a man of her own choosing. To be part of the Royal household of Egypt was considered an honour – a duty which superseded all personal needs or desires. She lay on her small bed. *Imagining.*

What would it be like, she wondered, to be a normal wife and mother. To be someone with her own life to lead, loved and loving? Her mind drifted back, back, to a hot summer day in the small village of her birth,

Chabria, beside the Nile. Once more she felt the hot sting of the sun on her arms, her constant thirst and the smell of the donkey dung rising in the steamy heat from the earth.

How very young she had been then, and not just in the number of years she had lived. How naive in the ways of the world. She drifted back into the sounds of her childhood.

—

The donkey slipped a little, its sure footedness betraying it under the heavy load it carried stacked onto its back.

'Hold the load steady, Amunet!'

'Yes, father, I will not let it fall!'

It had been a long, tiring day for the young girl just blossoming into womanhood. Her worn, dirt stained dress was drenched in sweat in the excruciating heat of the mid day sun. All day she had struggled to lift the life giving water to the crops using the shadoof on the banks of the Nile, or loading the donkey with the produce they had harvested.

Their family had been blessed with only one son to share the heavy work with her father. Despite the earnest prayers of her mother at the Temple to the goddess, Hathor, three daughters, of which she was the eldest, had been born to the family, but no more sons.

'This is the last load, Amunet,' said her father. 'Its time to finish for the day. You must feed the donkey and let it drink as soon as we are home.'

Amunet knew her father was worried. The waters of the Nile had once again not risen high enough on the nilometer to properly flood the plains this season providing the life giving black soil which enriched the fields. They would have insufficient food for the next harvest.

This was the third such year in a row and her family would struggle to survive. Tomorrow was market day. Hopefully they could barter what they had for some of what they needed.

Her parents' hope was that her brother could find a training position as a scribe – a much sought after, secure profession. Although the training was long and difficult with little reward until he had mastered the work under a master scribe's direction, once that had been completed, his future success would be assured.

The prices paid by even lowly Egyptians was high for personalised works by scribes of the Book of the Dead. Her brother should do well. Life, however, did not seem to be about to offer any such hope for Amunet or her sisters.

In that, however, she had been proven wrong.

She had been listening with interest to the raised voices from the house opposite, a few days after the market day.

'You will not darken the doorway of this house again, do you hear me until you stop visiting that harlot!' she heard their neighbour Alia yelling.

'I'll visit her as often as I like and there's nothing you can do about it!' her husband yelled back at her.

A knock came to the door of Arsinoe's family home at that point. Her father, opening the door, found a well dressed slave who handed him a scroll then left. The scroll read:

> *It has come to the notice of this Court, that your eldest daughter, Amunet, shows excellence in her supervision and disciplining of the younger children of your family when they are left in her care at the markets. You are requested to present her to the Royal Court of Alexandria at mid afternoon in two days time. You will ask for Ganymedes.*
>
> *The High Chancellor*
> *The Royal Palace of Alexandria*

Amunet's thoughts returned to the present. Her presentation at court had seen her accepted and trained in the care of the young Princess Arsinoe. She had been in her service ever since.

The consequences of the Battle of Alexandria had been horrific. Cleopatra, by succeeding in seducing and forming a pact with Caesar had, despite her hybrid bloodline, managed to banish Arsinoe to the sidelines of history, - unless she fought to take and hold, Egypt's throne.

Amunet remembered the events of the battle well. After the death of Achillas, Arsinoe and Ganymede's forces had fought well, only to be caught in a vice between the soldiers of Mithridates who had surprised them by arriving unexpectedly upon the scene, and those of Caesar.

Ptolemy, dismissed from the Royal Palace by Caesar after the death of Potheinus and sent back to the forces opposing the Romans, - died in the battle. Arsinoe by virtue of her pure royal bloodline, now considered herself, as did many others, the true Queen of Egypt.

The beautiful library of Alexandria had been completely consumed by the devastating fire spreading from the harbour, and with it, the world's most treasured intellectual heritage. Caesar had ordered the Egyptian fleet burned, and a flaming masthead had fallen onto the docks. The fire spread quickly, and could not be contained in time. Flames and smoke lit up the whole of Alexandria. The largest and most precious library In the world was utterly destroyed.

Arsinoe, after her defeat, was dragged before Caesar and Cleopatra at the Royal Palace. Treated with contempt by both, she was held as a prisoner at Caesar's pleasure. When he left Egypt he took Arsinoe with him as his prize captive for a Roman Triumphal parade to be followed by execution.

Caesar left Cleopatra on the throne with her new husband, her only remaining, younger brother, - which could be considered something akin to leaving a spider to devour a fly!

ANCIENT CITY OF APHRODISIAS

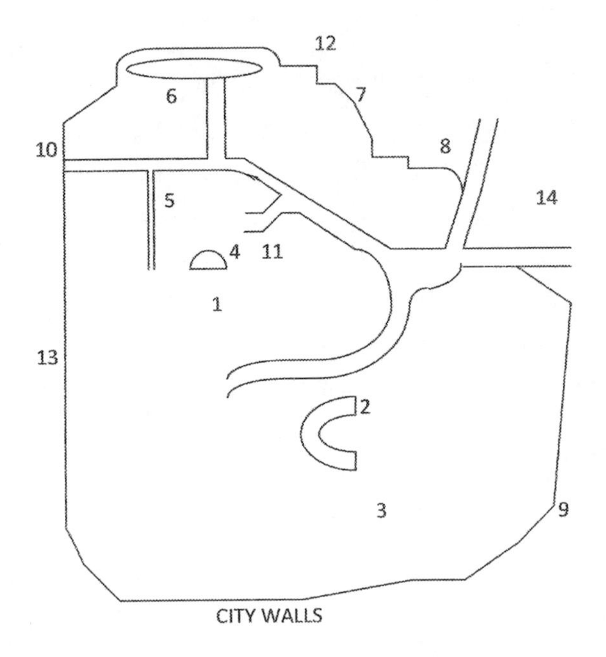

1. Agora
2. Theatre
3. Baths
4. Theatre (small)
5. Temple of Aphrodite
6. Stadium
7. North- East Gate
8. Side Gate
9. East Gate
10. West Gate
11. Sculptor's Shop
12. North Necropolis
13. West Necropolis
14. East Necropolis

*Map not to scale

Chapter 14

Aphrodisias

He wasn't quite sure when the idea first occurred to him really, but, when it did, he was astounded that he hadn't thought of it earlier. Sargon stretched out his aching legs and rubbed at the stiffness which for some hours had been creeping across his neck and shoulders. For a long journey inland such as this, he had decided not to ride alone but instead to travel in one of the jolting rather uncomfortable, cart like conveyances that passed for upper class travel.

Anyway! His mind went back to his previous thoughts. He needed to further broaden his prostitution business. Recently, he had added an extra house of 'pleasure' in Ephesus, but it was now time to expand out to other cities. He would hire managers and open other houses somewhere else for a trial, to see if his plan was workable.

Not wanting to be too far from his Ephesus base, he had decided upon the well known cities of Aphrodisias and Hierapolis which were quite close to each other. Right now, though, after long days of travel, often jolting along rough tracks, he wondered if it had been such a good idea after all.

The first rays of the rising sun turned Aphrodisias to gold and enchanted him. The small, walled city was beautiful. Built of marble on flat ground it was surrounded by trees as well as open countryside with hills in the distance. He made his way on the northern side to the large Agora.

'Is this where the markets are held?' he asked one of the locals standing nearby.

'This is usually where we hold our musical events. If you want to stay and listen you might even hear some really enthusiastic speakers as well.' The local man looked at Sargon with interest.

Strolling further around Aphrodisias, Sargon saw men at work in what appeared to be the centre of the city, building an enormous temple. Spectators stood around watching as the artisans worked on the Ionic columns and statues. He had been told previously that this city was dedicated to the goddess Aphrodite, the goddess of love. Looking at the city had seemed to him to be a worthwhile idea to pursue, given his business interests.

To the north lay a stadium capable he estimated of seating around 30,000 spectators. On enquiring, he was informed that mainly sporting events were held there. Or, of course, one could visit the Senate House which was also a roofed theatre. Walking over to the council chambers he spoke to an official looking man somewhat formally dressed.

'Good morning. Would you mind telling me a little about your beautiful city?' he asked.

'This is a city of the arts. It's only small as yet, but we have every cultural type of entertainment anyone could want.'

Sargon smiled. It wasn't exactly cultural entertainment he had in mind. The official noticed his hesitation.

'Of course, if it's some type of sport that you would like, or even chariot races, we have plenty of that as well." He said, looking encouraging. 'We also make wonderful sculptures.'

'My name is Probus.' He led Sargon to the opposite side of the street. 'We are passing by the school of sculpture. They are famous for the quality of their beautiful statues and busts.' He nodded a greeting to the owner. 'You can see for yourself the artistry of the pieces, you won't find better anywhere.' He motioned to Sargon. 'Would you like to come in?' Probus was obviously proud of his city. Sargon was always on the lookout for any 'special' items that would set his home apart from others, so he decided to take a look.

He walked through the workshop inspecting the sculptors' work. The quality was superb, and the marble, flawless, he agreed. One of these pieces would certainly look impressive in his garden back in Ephesus. He ran his hands lingeringly over the curves of a particularly sensual statue of Aphrodite. 'I will buy this one.' He gave the owner delivery arrangements, then continued on with his guide.

Slowing their steps they took advantage of the shade from the poplar and pomegranate trees, then walked to the crossroads, passing through the Tetrapylon with its ornately decorated reliefs of Eros and Nike. Its four rows of four graceful columns connected it to the Sacred Way leading to the construction site of the new Temple of Aphrodite. Sargon was impressed. Probus smiled across at him.

'We could do with just a few more new people moving here. Not too many, you understand, we don't want to become as large as a place like Ephesus, but at the moment we are probably a little too limited in our population.'

'Thank you. I'm just visiting at the moment, but I will think about it.' Sargon replied.

Theatre, sculpture, philosophy and music all flourished here. This, Sargon concluded, was not really the type of city he was looking for.

The pursuits sought by its citizens were predominantly of an intellectual, cultural or sporting nature, and brothels in the city would probably not prove profitable enough also, intuition told him they practised sacred prostitution. Still, he was glad he had come. Aphrodisias was a place to be appreciated, business or not. It was beautiful enough, he thought, to indeed be the city of love. But what would he know about that? The only thing he had ever really experienced was closer to lust. He stretched his cramped limbs and after an overnight stay, set out for Hierapolis.

ANCIENT CITY OF HIERAPOLIS

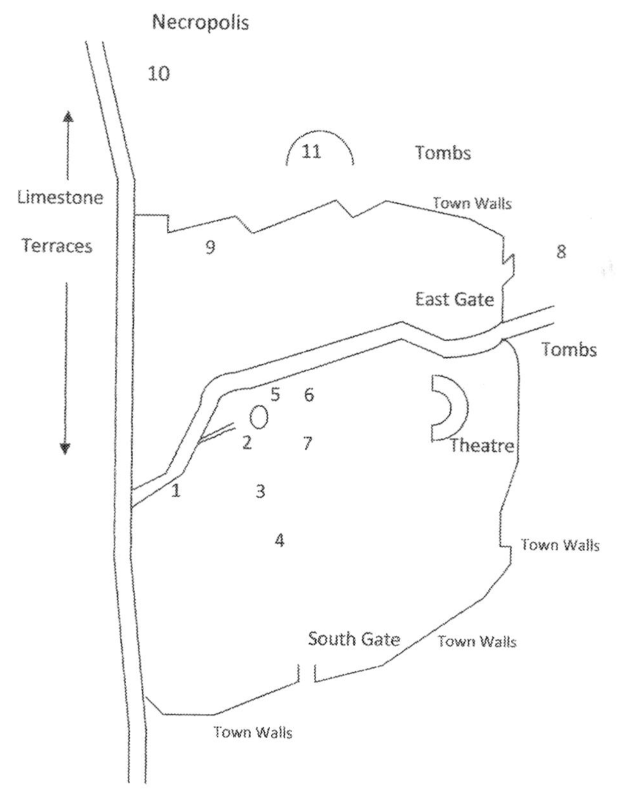

1. Great Baths
2. Sacred Pool
3. Agora
4. Sculptor's Workshop
5. Nymphaeum
6. Temple of Apollo
7. Plutonium
8. Cistern
9. Basilica
10. Northern Baths
11. Theatre (small)

Chapter 15

Hierapolis

Sargon's first sighting of the gleaming, white hillside of the limestone spa area beside which Hierapolis had been built, was enough to dispel any doubts. A vast expanse of pure, white terraces, glistening in the sun, under a blue sky, met his eyes.

Sargon had been told that people came for miles to cure their aches and illnesses here in the thermal springs. What better place, he thought, for one of his higher class brothels to deal with their other 'urges' and needs as well?

Approaching the city he paid off his driver and walked the remaining, short distance to an impressive, arched entry gate that stood before him - one of several entrances to the walled city. He knew little about Hierapolis, the 'sacred' city so called because of its many temples. One thing he did know, however, was that it took money to come to such a place for a cure to the many ailments people suffered, and money, meant business!

For the next three days he acquainted himself with the layout of the city, and availed himself of the hot springs and the best brothel he could find. Passing by the sculptors' workshop, he admired their work and stopped to chat with the owner. 'How is business these days? Are people spending much?'

The workshop owner, looking at the fine cut of Sargon's clothes and thinking he might have a new customer, was inclined to be talkative. 'I can't complain! Best lot of orders we've had for a long time! As long as they keep dying too, we'll have a lot more, especially for headstones.'

He nodded in the direction of one of the many large necropolis areas outside the city walls.

'They come here with the daft idea of walking away cured. But, as you can see, most of them have ended up dead!' He gave a grim chuckle.

'What's your business, anyway?'

'I'm looking to set up some new city brothels.' Sargon lowered his voice confidentially.

The shop owner grinned.

'Well, when you're ready, come and see me for a nice statue or bust for your house of business.'

With that, he turned away to inspect the nearest commissioned piece being worked on by one of his artisans. The quality was questionable. Sargon wandered over to the nearest Necropolis. It lay near the east gate of the city, outside the walls.

Many of the names on the headstones were Jewish, with varying dates of death covering some decades, or unreadable. Tufts of grass grew in and between the graves which were of many shapes and sizes, some obviously for children. A few featured ornate scrolls decorated in an expensive fashion.

Several were actually leaning sideways with age, caked with the mould of time, whilst others were tall and straight. They stood like sentinels to – who knew where?

Although some were well tended, many were neglected. Some headstones were cracked and disintegrating after decades of battering by rain and wind. Sargon shuddered, the decay and finality of the place scared him.

He stood watching a couple of grave diggers bending their backs under the noon day sun. Dressed in filthy rags, they were preparing a hole for the next body.

'Has someone just died?' Sargon enquired

'No. This one's for whoever dies next.' The older of the two men laughed grimly as he replied.

'May the other gods help him then.' Sargon shook his head. 'Because it looks like Apollo won't!'

Muttering to himself, he turned quickly away and made his way back to the city of the living.

Sargon's enquiries from suppliers for the goods he would need and the purchase of a suitable premises went well. He had, he thought, chosen a very good location. He needed somewhere quite central, but where there would not be too much competition from other entertainment distractions.

The city's population was around half that of Ephesus, but the facilities were excellent, with a large theatre that had a particularly beautiful stage area. The front row of seats was especially reserved for the wealthy and officials.

On his first night in Hierapolis Sargon had attended a performance, sitting up towards the back along with other citizens of no particular importance. He had waited until everyone had gone.

The night was still and quiet, with a full moon casting an eerie light onto the stage. He walked up to the front row and sat down in the premier seat, right in the middle.

'With any luck I will be sitting in this seat during a performance one day.' Sargon said softly to himself.

He had actually enjoyed himself immensely, - even in the 'cheap' seats. He had chosen a good night to attend as the play being performed, *'Miles Gloriosus'* by the Roman playwright, Titus Plautus, was set somewhere he was very much at home, - Ephesus. Even better, the play was a comedy about a bragging soldier, which suited his mood. It was exaggerated in nature with the usual stock characters, and succeeded in drawing much laughter from the audience.

As with the majority of plays it was spoken in Latin but the actors, poor maligned creatures that they usually were, wore Greek clothes, wigs and stage paint which must have taken no one knew how long to apply, and even longer to take off! One career Sargon knew he certainly did not want to pursue, - was the theatre!

The city of Hierapolis also enjoyed a choice of baths to attend. He envisioned years of prosperity ahead with the capacity for the growth of a new chain of his brothels, which would allow him to live in splendour for the rest of his days. He had no intention of ending up old, sick and poor.

By night he wandered the streets keeping watch on the number of customers visiting the two brothels he had found. On his last evening in the city, Sargon was making his way past the Temple of Apollo, when without warning, he found himself confronted by three large men in front of him. Turning to retrace his steps in the dark, he realised fearfully that others were also behind him.

'Here, take my money. You can also have everything else I have with me,' he bargained.

'No need for that,' smiled one of his assailants. 'You shouldn't be stepping on turf that's not your own. Do you get my meaning? Word is around that you plan to take over the brothel business. Now, that just wouldn't do, would it?'

Struggling desperately, Sargon was forcibly dragged to the edge of the sacred pool between the columns, where his head was submerged, shoved hard under the waters of Apollo and held there. He died gasping for air, providing yet another headstone order for the owner of the sculptors' workshop.

PART IV

'A human being is only breath and shadow.'

Sophocles

Chapter 16

EPHESUS
The Temple of Artemis

The citizens of Ephesus were barely opening their eyes from sleep when a detachment of Roman soldiers marched from their barracks near the harbour, into Marble Street, then up Curetes Street, their boots ringing out a sharp rhythm on the paving stones. A fine mist drizzled down on them from the last of the rain clouds now retreating across the sky. The Centurion's face was set in a grim line, his breastplate gleaming and his steps firm. But these soldiers were not heading for a city trouble spot. They were heading for a place of peace.

There was a gentle tapping on Arsinoe's door and the Megabyzus softly called her name. Having bathed and dressed earlier, she responded quickly to his summons. 'You are requested to come with me to the visiting area,' he said.

Her hopes rose – perhaps Octavian had at last sent a messenger.

As she reached the front reception area of the Temple she realised her mistake. The Centurion in charge stepped forward.

'My Lady, Arsinoe, you will accompany us out of the Temple!'

In desperation Arsinoe pleaded with the High Priest. 'If I leave the Temple they will kill me!' His eyes met hers in pity.

'My Lady, I cannot help you. The order is signed by the Governor, Marcus Antonius, and I cannot risk other innocent lives. It is useless to resist.'

Arsinoe turned to face the Centurion.

'You will wait until I have prayed to the goddess!'

With that, she turned and walked slowly to a side shrine to Isis, where she sank to her knees. She had faced death once before in the Roman Tullianum prison and beaten it. This time, however, she knew was final. She prayed that when her heart was weighed by Anubis on the scales at the moment of reckoning after the great voyage of the soul after death, her deeds would not be found wanting.

Arsinoe rose and, head high, using every ounce of courage she possessed, she walked towards the entry. The Centurion came towards her. She looked into his eyes.

'Curse Antony and my whore of a sister through Eternity!' she screamed.

Quickly he sank the gladius into her heart. Arsinoe lost her life staggering forward, run through with a soldier's gladius. She fell onto the marble steps her long black hair fanning out around her.

The Hippodrome
The Mithraeum

A flash of gold, shiny and jewelled. Black hair flying into his face. Blood everywhere! The sticky wetness clung to his hands and smeared his arms. Still her scream rang in his ears! And her courage shamed him! Valerius woke in a cold sweat. His head pounded and he groaned as the reality of the events of the day before hit him. That was not a soldier's duty, - it should have been the job of an assassin.

How would his men feel this morning after dragging a defenceless, beautiful young woman from the religious refuge of the Temple to murder her? As the Centurion in charge, it had been his gladius which had sunk deep into the girl's flesh, forever silencing her. He had taken responsibility for the act rather than giving the order to one of his men. Now he waited for them to assemble for the day's roster.

He looked around the group in front of him. Most were battle hardened veterans who had seen duty in places like Gaul. None would look into another's eyes today though, for fear of what they might see there. Proud Roman Centurion though he was, Valerius nonetheless understood the shame that yesterday's actions had brought upon them all.

'We are rostered today at the Hippodrome, so, as the duties are light, we should all be able to enjoy the chariot races. For those of you who feel the need, however, I will be going first to the Mithraeum. I suggest we go as a group.' There were grunts of assent and nods all round. 'We will meet underneath the Hippodrome one hour before the usual time.' With that he dismissed them.

The Hippodrome was well located to accommodate the entertainment it offered. Built well away from the central area of the city but still easily accessible at the very end of Marble Street, it stood on the same side of the street as the great Theatre, past the turning to Arcadian Street.

Most of the population of Ephesus enjoyed Roman style leisure pursuits. It was just a matter of finding a patron or sponsor willing to provide the money to run the events. In the case of the chariot racing, the costs could be considerable.

The chariot races were always popular and crowded. The entry was through a magnificent monumental entrance gate which added to the feeling of a special occasion and heightened the excitement. Although not in any way a match for the great Circus Maximus in Rome, the Ephesus venue held 13,000 and the noise, heightened by excitement and betting was huge. Valerius and his men after entering well before starting time, however, walked underneath the area housing the behind the scenes activities, to the rear of the arched starting gates. They headed for a little known opening hidden in shadow.

They entered into the dark recesses of the Mithraeum cut into the rocks well below ground level. Cave-like, quiet and dim, it provided an appropriately aesthetic setting for the ceremony they were about to undertake. Valerius hoped that it would help to lessen the impact of last night's horror.

Mithras, the god of soldiers represented the values of duty, honour and sacrifice. The religion had its roots in the Persian god of light and wisdom. Mithras was represented on a central altar dragging a bull and then cutting its throat. Stone benches lined the sides of the cavern. The setting was austere, but suited to the followers of this cult religion.

An animal was sacrificed and the blood allowed to drain into the opening provided at the side underneath the floor. The communal meal which followed, formed part of the ceremony which joined the soldiers together and strengthened their common sense of duty.

'We have paid due homage today to Mithras,' said Valerius at the conclusion. 'We also acknowledge that it can be difficult at times to do our duty. May this ceremony today ease the load we are carrying.'

Then they walked out into the light.

The procession preceding the opening of that day's events had already begun, and the Senior Senator sponsoring the chariot races had passed through the ceremonial entry gate with the charioteers and teams following close behind.

'Separate and mix with the crowd so you can quieten down any troublemakers. Just keep an eye on that group on the far right, - things are getting out of hand early there,' ordered Valerius, watching a group of young spectators who had just started a brawl. It looked as if the follower of the green team was getting well on top of his rival blue follower. 'We'll meet outside the entry gate just before the twelfth race to cover the exits as everyone leaves!'

Each team of four horses carried their own colours – red, green, white, or blue shown by the colour of the charioteer's tunic. Wearing helmets and arm protectors, the drivers, usually slaves, were strong, their muscles straining to control the highly spirited horses. Racing chariots were lightweight and fast, unlike war chariots, but offered little protection.

Betting was still going on at a furious pace amongst the crowd and every class of citizen in Ephesus could be seen shouting to place his bet.

'I'll give you three to one on the red team!' yelled one supporter.

'What, do you think I'm stupid? The last time I came here with you I went home with nothing!' shouted his companion good naturedly.

The clamour from the crowd reached fever pitch as the trumpets blared and the priests arrived carrying statues of Jupiter and other gods. The teams headed to the carceres gates. Those unlucky enough to draw the outside positions at least got the benefit of a staggered start. The teams lined up in front of the entry gates and entered the stadium to drive one lap of honour around the central spina. Then they stood behind the starting gates. Waiting.

Proclaiming the glory of Ephesus and the Empire, the Senior Senator gave the usual, expected speech. He also paid homage to the drivers, who came from a variety of different places, amongst them this day, Carthage, Rome and Corinth, as well as a local driver born in Ephesus, who had trained in Rome. It had taken much organisation and money to arrange the cartage of all the horses, chariots and drivers to the city.

The cry rang out '*Watch the line! Watch the line*!' and the assistants holding the front of the horses ran for cover as the white cloth signalling the start dropped to the ground. Swirls of dust flew, rising over the crowd in a haze, as the sound of the horses hooves thundered through the Stadium and they jostled for position round the first turn. The first dolphin on the spina was turned downwards as the second lap began. The race length was seven laps of the stadium.

The events were expected to move along quickly and smoothly. Even so, it took considerable time to run all seven laps. Those removing injured or dead drivers and horses from the course were in considerable danger themselves. Simply for self preservation, if nothing else, they moved quickly before the horses swept down upon them again. It would, however, be late into the afternoon before all events had finished.

The charioteers were soon covered in dirt and sweat and some with blood as they were injured in falls with horses coming together violently, or knocking against the central spina. All 13,000 spectators were on their feet cheering as the victors came forward after each race to receive their palm branches and laurel wreaths.

One of the two most popular sports in the Roman Empire was part of the way of life in Ephesus. It was considered by those in high authority as a good way of keeping everyone out of trouble.

Chapter 17

ROME
The Curia (Senate House)

Agrippa had made his way up to the Palatine to Octavian's villa to walk with him back to the Senate meeting scheduled for that morning. He was not prepared for the state he found Octavian in when he got there.

'He's gone too far this time, Marcus! I'll have his head for this!'

Agrippa had never seen Octavian quite so furious. His features had twisted into a snarl and his hands were balled into fists.

'That Egyptian slut he's with will die with him!' he snapped.

'What's Antonius done this time?' Agrippa enquired mildly as they left the villa for the Senate House.

'You'll see soon enough!' Octavian glowered and he refused to be drawn further on the subject, so they continued their walk in silence.

Standing in the centre of the Senate Chamber, Octavian re- arranged the folds of his toga and waited for complete silence. Then he raised his hand in the air, waving a scroll. 'Do you know what this is my friends?' he shouted. 'This is a message from the Megabyzus of Ephesus. And do you know what it says? No? How could you know? How could you possibly imagine that any Roman would break Rome's traditions so flagrantly.

This message informs us that despite being offered safe refuge in the Temple of Artemis by none other than Caesar himself, Princess Arsinoe was murdered in the Temple! And you may ask, - *By whom was she murdered?* My fellow Senators, she was executed by the order of Marcus Antonius, Autocrator of the East!'

Complete chaos broke out in the chamber. When the roar of disapproval had died down, Octavian continued. 'The Temple of Artemis is dedicated to the Goddess Artemis, know to us as the Roman Goddess Diana. The tradition of safe refuge has never before been violated. You may ask why would a noble Roman such as Antonius do such a thing? Why would he show such disrespect for our religion? I give you the answer – He was ordered to do it by his Egyptian whore, Cleopatra!'

Any hope of continuing the meeting disappeared as Senators shouted at each other or sat in stunned silence. Octavian walked out.

Agrippa found himself wondering why the incident had upset Octavian quite so much. His thoughts went back to the day the messenger had brought Arsinoe's message to Rome. Now just what had been in that message?

EPHESUS
Late 41BC

The day dawned with a rosy hued sky as delicate as a cherub's smile. Slowly, the sleepy city of Ephesus awoke to the perfection of a gentle breeze and warming sunshine. The augur's sacrificial rites performed earlier, foretold good fortune for the city's citizens. There was something special, however, a certain 'feeling' those who were there this day, said later. It was a stillness, as if destiny had closed a chapter. It was the right sort of day, if such a thing exists, to bury a Princess. Many would have said that Arsinoe was a Queen.

Her body was carried on a bier high on the shoulders of the priests as the procession moved slowly from the portico of the Temple of Artemis down the long, last mile towards the gates of the city of Ephesus.

A silent, but surprisingly large gathering of local citizens, among them Amunet, leaning against Lucius for support, stood waiting for Arsinoe's arrival. Her murder in the Temple, a place of refuge, was thought by most to be in violation of the protection guaranteed in the sanctuary of the Goddess Artemis.

Valerius and his men were not needed. There would not be any violence on this day. They attended, however, and stood watching over the scene. Eventually, the procession reached its destination.

'She was only really just a girl.' One of his men spoke softly to Valerius.

'No, Claudius,' he replied.

'She wasn't just a girl. She was a young woman of beauty and great courage!'

They stood before the rectangular Temple of Isis in the Upper Agora. Arsinoe had expressed a wish to have the last ritual performed there should the gods call her to them. The Megabyzus had respected and carried out her wishes.

At the stele by the entrance to the Temple the body was ceremonially passed to the shaven haired, white robed priests of Isis, who carried Arsinoe through the doors and into a side preparation room. There her body was anointed with myrrh and rubbed with aromatic oils before she was once again dressed in her long, white robe.

She wore a gold snake bracelet on her upper arm, a golden circlet in her hair and a heavy gold Egyptian necklace. Her face, serene in the candle light was truly beautiful. As requested by Amunet, the final adornment, was the application of her favourite perfume, the blue lotus.

The interior of the temple was dim and cool. A statue to the goddess Isis stood in a central shrine. Hieroglyphs decorated the pillars, while engravings of Isis surrounded them on the walls, along with papyrus and lotus flowers. The sistrums could be heard along with an ancient, melancholy chanting – while, over all, hung the pervasive scent of the incense.

Silence reigned as the High Priest proceeded with the ritual. No one who attended that day ever forgot the experience. Arsinoe's tomb stood waiting for her nearby.

Hers had been a short, but remarkable life.

—

Antony and Cleopatra's massive, largely Egyptian fleet lay peacefully at anchor as they swept into Ephesus up Arcadian Street and turned left, headed for the Governor's Palace. It was located past the Theatre on the other side of Marble Street. Some would say that, apart from the hippodrome located some distance away, it was at the quiet end, away from the hustle and bustle of Curetes Street.

Having settled into the palace and enjoyed refreshments they decided to leave with their retinue to shop, explore and visit the famed Temple of

Artemis. They admired the great Theatre and the beauty of Marble Street, as well as the famous Library.

As they walked Curetes Street, an impressive octagonal tomb 50 feet high with papyrus columns and topped with a pyramid caught Cleopatra's attention.

'Whose tomb is that?' She enquired from Antony, though in truth she already thought she knew, for the shape of the tomb echoed that of the great Pharos Lighthouse of Alexandria.

'I think you know.' He replied. 'I hope I have fulfilled your request as you desired.'

Cleopatra smiled up at him.

'Well, little sister,' she said softly to herself. 'Finally I am rid of you!' Then she went on her way without as much as a backward glance.

EPILOGUE

EGYPT
Outside Alexandria
Tabusiris Magna Temple
The Present Day

LIGHT FILTERS THROUGH the tiny cell window and the shadows creep across the room once more. No human voice or footfall has disturbed this place for centuries. Silence.

Day by day the sun god Re Herakhty sweeps across the sky. The lonely casket in its wall niche has long since disintegrated in the stillness. Sand covers the window and all is darkness. The temple is lost in a mantle of shifting sand.

In the cell one object remains, dusty with the passing of generations, - an ancient signet ring, - it bears the name '*Alexander*.' Worn by a conqueror revered by others considered heroes in their own time and beyond, - Caesar, Octavian, Antony, Napoleon, - none has yet been found worthy to wear this ultimate seal of greatness.

A sound reaches the cell. It is the melody of a human voice. Soon it is joined by the sensation of human hands digging through the sands. Perhaps it is time at last.

Perhaps.

AN ANCIENT CURSE COMES TO PASS

ARSINOE'S CURSE FOLLOWED Cleopatra and Antony through the years until their own desperate deaths. After their defeat at the Battle of Actium on 2nd September, BC 31 each died by their own hand. Over two thousand years later, Arsinoe's tomb remains, and is visited by thousands of travellers passing through Ephesus. The tombs of Antony and Cleopatra lie undiscovered.

Caesarion was murdered by Octavian

THE TOMB OF ARSINOE
EPHESUS, TURKEY

The octagonal tomb of Arsinoe IV of Egypt was identified in Ephesus in the 1990's.

Ephesus is estimated to have been ten times larger than the city of Pompeii. Only five tombs are located within the city walls. Arsinoe's tomb is the only one belonging to a female. It is located in central Curetes Street.

Built in the shape of the Pharos Lighthouse, Alexandria, it was 50 feet high, with papyrus shaped pillars and topped with a round orb. Nothing else similar has been found in Ephesus. Carbon dating of the skeleton confirmed the dating of the tomb.

The remains of the tomb can be visited by travellers to Ephesus.

Reference: BBC Television Documentary *Cleopatra: Portrait of a Killer*. 2009

Tomb of Arsinoe IV of Egypt. Curetes Street, Ephesus, Turkey.

Photo: J. Blundell

The Author

Lorraine Blundell (Parsons) was born in Brisbane, Australia in 1946. She has a son, Steven, and a daughter, Jennilee. Lorraine lives in Melbourne, Australia. She holds a Bachelor of Arts Degree from the University of Queensland majoring in English and History, and a teaching qualification in Drama from Trinity College, London.

From 1960 to 1966 Lorraine trained in singing at the Queensland State Conservatorium of Music. Spanning that period she had a professional television career as a regular solo vocalist singing on numerous entertainment and variety programs, both State and National, for television channels BTQ 7 and QTQ 9 Brisbane, and HSV 7 Melbourne. She has also performed on stage in amateur musical theatre productions.

Her passions are singing, ancient history and archaeology and she has travelled extensively. This is her first novel.

Author's Notes

Fact and Fiction

Arsinoe of Ephesus is fiction based strongly on historical fact. Some timelines, events and places have been changed to suit the plot.

The Library of Celsus

The famous Library of Celsus was completed in approximately AD 135.

Some other structures in the novel were also completed after Arsinoe's death.

The Temple of Artemis, Ephesus

One of the seven wonders of the ancient world. A place of refuge for rich political exiles. Arsinoe was exiled for life to the Temple by Caesar, who pardoned her from her death sentence.

The unsuccessful assassination attempt in the Temple of Artemis

There is no known record of such a first assassination attempt in the Temple.

The Cult of Mithras

Mithras was the god of soldiers. An ancient cult probably originating from Persia, it was popular with Roman soldiers and Mithraic sites have been found in Rome. It is not known if the same was the case in Ephesus.

The Execution of Arsinoe

Arsinoe was executed on the steps of the Temple of Artemis by the order of Mark Antony as a favour to Cleopatra in BC41. Antony was Autocrator of the East, and Governor of Ephesus.

Caesar's Egyptian Triumph

Arsinoe was paraded in the triumph after waging the war of Alexandria against Caesar who had formed a pact with Cleopatra in Alexandria.

The welcome of the High Priest of the Temple to Arsinoe as 'Queen'

The High Priest was reprimanded by Cleopatra for using the title when admitting Arsinoe to the Temple. A delegation had to visit Cleopatra with an apology.

Alexander's Signet Ring

Alexander the Great is thought by many historians to have been buried in a tomb in the Brucheion district in Alexandria. As the last of the pure blooded Ptolemy line it is not impossible that Arsinoe may have had his ring, but we do not know. Cleopatra was considered of "hybrid" blood.

Arsinoe's conspiracy with Octavian

There is no known record of such an agreement.

Senate disapproval after Arsinoe's murder

The Roman Senate is said to have been in an uproar when informed of Arsinoe's murder. The violation of the sanctuary of the Temple was considered unforgivable.

Cleopatra and Antony's visit to Arsinoe's tomb

In late BC 41 Cleopatra and Antony visited Ephesus.

The Library of Pergamon

The second largest library in the known world, after Alexandria. Marc Antony stripped the Library of its scrolls to give to Cleopatra as a wedding present.

Glossary

A

Amphorae (Pl) Vessel made of pottery with two handles usually used for carrying wine or wheat.

Amun Amun-Ra. An Egyptian god. Champion of the poor, and personal piety.

Antigone A Greek tragedy written by Socrates. The third of three Theban plays

B

Basilica A public building which contained shops and offices

C

Cacat! An exclamation. Shit!

Carcer A dungeon, usually a one roomed upper section. Rome had no State prison as such.

Centurion A professional soldier. An officer in a roman or auxiliary legion.

Circus The place where chariot races were held. The central area was called the Spina. Dolphins in the central area were used to show the number of laps completed, usually out of a total of seven.

Curia Rome. The Senate House

D

Dolia A large vessel, often six feet high with a flat bottom but without handles. Used to carry various merchandise especially by ship.

F

Forum Romanum The Roman Forum. The centre of activities in Rome. The area in which all important buildings were located, including the Senate House, and important public speeches given.

Friend and Ally of Rome A title given to those rulers who enjoyed particularly friendly and allied status with Rome.

G

Gladiator Professional warrior. Often slaves, occasionally free men. Performed for the entertainment of the people, usually in a stadium or colosseum.

Gladius Roman sword used by soldiers, 25-32 inches long.

H

Horus A major Egyptian god. Usually considered the god of the sky and shown as a falcon.

I

Impluvium A square basin in the middle of an Atrium. Used to catch rain water from an open space in the roof.

Insulae (Pl) Apartment buildings housing many people, usually the poor.

Isis Egyptian goddess of major importance. Wife of Osiris and mother of Horus. Goddess of motherhood, love and magic.

K

Ka Life force or 'spirit.'

L

Litter Used to carry usually one or two people. It could be carried by four men using the horizontal poles attached to the covered cubicle.

M

Megabyzus The Head Priest of the Temple of Artemis, Ephesus.

Mithras The god of soldiers. Believed to have strong Persian roots. Represented honour and duty. Usually worshipped in underground caverns cut out of rock having a central altar and seats lining the cavern sides.

Morituri Te Salutant We who are about to die salute you.

P

Patricians Romans belonging to the elite social class.

Peristyle Courtyard garden area.

Pharos Lighthouse Alexandria, Egypt. One of the seven ancient wonders of the world. It stood at the entrance to the harbour.

Philae Temple Ancient Egyptian Temple dedicated to the goddess, Isis. Situated on an island. Near the city of Aswan.

Plutarch Roman historian AD 45-145, famous for his biographies of great Romans.

Pontifex Maximus Head priest of the Roman State religion.

Q

Quinquereme A large Roman transport galley with five oars on each side.

S

Serapis An Egyptian god with roots in Alexandria. A god of the lower classes.

T

Tabusiris Magna Temple Just outside the city of Alexandria, Egypt. Presently under excavation by archaeologists.

Tace Shut up!

Temple of Artemis In Ephesus, Turkey. One of the seven wonders of the ancient world. Built on swampy land and has not survived. A huge temple dedicated to the worship of the Mother goddess of fertility, Artemis (Roman goddess Diana). Well known refuge for rich political exiles.

Triumph Aspired to by every successful Roman General. A celebratory parade of victory which travelled through the Forum. A triumph could only be granted by the Roman Senate.

Triumvirate A Roman political arrangement, formal or informal, between three powerful leaders.

Tullianum One room of a two storied prison building of which this was the lower section where prisoners were strangled then their bodies thrown into the sewer.

V

Vesta Important Roman goddess of the hearth. Particularly important to the home. Usually, a perpetual flame was kept burning in the place where she was honoured.

Vestal Virgins Priestesses of Vesta, goddess of the hearth. They took a vow of chastity to devote themselves to religious rituals and could be executed for breaking their vows.

Via Appia Major Roman road built in 312BC The road ran from the port of Brundisium in the south to Rome.

Via Sacra The Sacred Way. The main street of Rome running from the Capitoline Hill through the Forum to the Colosseum.

BIBLIOGRAPHY

Blake P. & Blezard P. *The Arcadian Cipher*. P. 32,57. Pan Macmillan. 2001. London.

Plutarch. *Lives of the Noble Grecians and Romans*. V.5. (1579) London.

Strabo. *Geography*. 1.9. 17.1.11

Sophocles. Antigone. *BC 442*. Greece.

RECOMMENDED READING

George M. *Memoires of Cleopatra*. Pan Macmillan. London. 1997

Holland T. *Rubicon – The Triumph and Tragedy of the Roman Republic*. Little Brown. Great Britain. 2003

McCullough C. *Antony and Cleopatra*. Harper Collins. Australia. 2007

PHOTO GALLERY

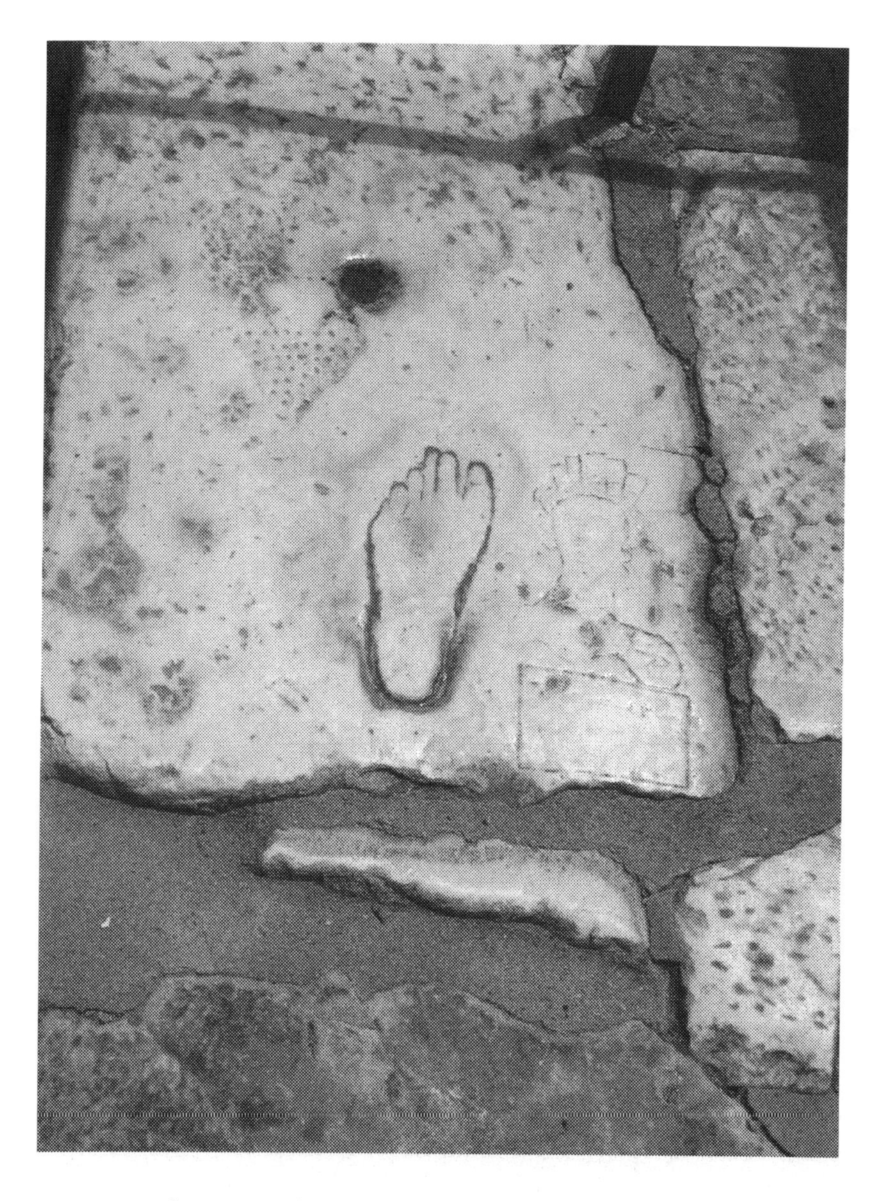

Ephesus, Turkey. Marble Street. Paving Slab with pictures of foot and prostitute.

Photo: J. Blundell

Rome. A Mithraeum.

Photo: J. Blundell

Ephesus, Turkey. Gates of Mazeus and Mithridates.

Photo: J. Blundell

Egypt. Temple of Isis. Philae.

Photo: J. Blundell

Ruins of the ancient Persian city of Sardis.

Photo: J. Blundell

Pergamon. Turkey. The Greek Theatre

Photo: J. Blundell

Aesklepion. Turkey.

Ancient Healing Centre. Patient Treatment Rooms.

Photo: J. Blundell

Hierapolis. Turkey. The Theatre

Photo: J. Blundell

A small hillside town outside Rome. Home town of Suetonius.

Photo: J. Blundell